? C r o p   C i r c l e s ?

? Crop Circles ?

*An Alien's
Middle School
Science Project*

By
Ken Renshaw

Constellation Press
Cambria, California
2016

Copyright

ISBN: 978-0-9616620-4-2

Cover design by Heather UpChurch

ACKNOWLEDGMENTS

I would like to thank Shawn Randall who was our tour guide of crop circle country in Wiltshire, England. She channeled Torah's insight into the mystery of the crop circles.

I thank my fellow writers, and Paula Cizmar at Rough Writers for their support and comments. Roxane Broderick's careful final editing amazed me. And special thanks to Heather UpChurch for her inspired cover design.

Constellation Press

1790 Ogden Dr.

Cambria. CA 93428

Contents

A Crop Circle

CHAPTER 1

The Earthlings 1a Course

I'm in the presence of great authority, I thought. I sat in the
office of my school principal, Dr. Oz, waiting to get my assignment
for my next stage of learning. This Earthlings Study assignment is
an important lesson because the Elders will use Dr. Oz's
recommendation in deciding my future track of lessons.

"Oh what a great adventure you're about to go on," said
Dr. Oz. "In your middle school Earthlings 1a course you will study
the illusion called Earth and its indigenous peoples."

Before I signed up for the courses, I had learned that Earth
is a planet on the Orion Arm of Galaxy 356. Locals call the galaxy
the Milky Way.

Dr. Oz was sitting behind a large oak desk, neat, with only
one paper in his inbox, resting on a green blotter. He looked like an
academic, wearing a worn tweed jacket with leather patches sewn
on the elbows.

"First ,we need to go over some rules." He handed me the
paper from his inbox. It read:

The Prime Directive, General Order #1, is the prominent
guiding principle of the United Federation of Galaxies. The Prime

Directive dictates that there can be no interference with the internal development of contacted Galaxies or planets.

All you can do is suggest things to the indigenous peoples to guide them in their life experience. You may alter physical phenomena only on small scales as part of your lesson to them.

On the planets that employ the illusion of time, you cannot change the sequence of events that are assigned time coordinates.

You may not transfer technology to them. You may direct their attention to ideas or technology that already exist in their society.

I read two more pages of more specific do's and don'ts and looked up at Dr. Oz.

"Do you understand the rules?" He asked.

"I understand the rules" I echoed

Dr. Oz smiled and said, "I don't want to seem as stern as the written rules. I want you to understand that this assignment is a responsible one, and you should ask for guidance before you venture near the bounds of those directives.

"Here is a Knowledge Plate from the Galaxy 356 records for you to use in learning about Earth," he continued. "It is an index of all the significant events for every individual in Earth space-time records for the epoch they identify by their time system as the past fifty thousand years."

"See me if you get in trouble or need serious advice. Otherwise, I will see you at your final presentation and oral exam. Mr. Ob will be your proctor."

Dr. Oz stood up, and I immediately rose and left his office.

His illusion of the administration building at our school was a one-story brick building, on a slight rise, in a large square with lawn on all sides. This day, there was the moist smell of fresh lawn clippings as I walked from the building.

When Dr. Oz summoned me, I found I was in his illusion, one I had not experienced before.

I will describe my life, not in my terms, but in your earth terms. Here, we do not have bodies as you know bodies. Everything here is somewhat like living in imagination. When I need to transport or use something like the Knowledge Plate Dr. Oz gave me, I create something you might call a body to carry the object around or work with it.

Meeting Mr. Ob was a different experience than the formality of visiting Dr. Oz's office; it was more like what Earthlings would call a friend and gaining a trusted associate. I followed a dirt path into a small clearing in the grove of ancient trees on our campus. The sunlight filtered in streams through the branches, birds sang, and creatures scampered in the leaves amid the shadows. The place had the pleasant smell of decaying wood. Mr. Ob was meditating cross-legged on a log, his face illuminated by a beam of light that streamed through the canopy. He wore a loose-fitting orange robe. He looked up as he heard me approach, nodded his hairless head, and beamed a smile at me.

I thought, *There is a sanctity about this place. It welcomes me.*

"I've been expecting you," he said in a soft voice. "Sit on this log across from me. I see you have the latest generation of the Knowledge Plate. Let me see it."

Since I was in the illusion of physical reality that Mr. Ob had created, I occupied the illusion of a body similar to his. I took the Knowledge Plate from under my arm and handed it to him.

Knowledge Plates are not hardware. Mine is a genetically engineered, living object. You might call it a neural network, contained in a skin-like tissue case. Our equivalent of your engineers created a ten-stranded DNA used to grow our devices. When we hold them in our hands, they process our thoughts and

3

display information in our mind's eye. In a sense, they are like your books in that they contain compartments of information. We can easily search through a subject such as Earth History.

"You'll use it in Earthlings 1a to learn to create illusions that appear like Earth's reality. I've bookmarked the subjects of your Earthlings 1a course. You'll learn Earth culture and to communicate with and understand a semi-merged pair of male-female energy units known as Dave and Raven. Here, join me in holding the tablet."

I joined Mr. Ob in holding the tablet and saw, in my mind's eye, a couple walking hand-in-hand in amidst a barren landscape. After I had watched for a while, I asked, "What is that strange growth from their heads?"

"Oh, those are protein strings that they call hair. It is ugly, but you will get used to it. They seem to take great pride in shaping it. The taller unit, the mostly male energy with the short hair, is called Dave. The longer haired shorter unit with very feminine energy is called Raven or Ravi.

"After you get to know, their energies and the life-lessons they are working on, come back and we will decide on a program of interaction. For your final part of Earthlings 1a course, you will design a science project which experiments with Earthling behavior."

I walked away, bubbling with excitement over my new Knowledge Plate and my assignment. Earth, and Earthlings Ravi and Dave, will be fun to study.

CHAPTER 2

Strange Earthling Behavior

My next meeting with Mr. Ob takes place in an Earth-like illusion I created of a cascading waterfall on our campus. Excuse me; I should have said took place. I'm still not used to your ideas of present and past, and the idea of time as you know it.

I have to learn how to relate things in the form of a story,because we don't have stories here, since time does not exist as you understand it, and your stories record things in time. You have places in your stories. We've scenes we mentally create to fit an interaction. Mr. Ob created the story of our first interaction. Here, I create the story of our second interaction.

As I walked through the deep forest on a dirt path, I heard the sound of a waterfall. When it appeared, I saw that it tumbled out of a high, black stone cliff onto a bed of enormous black boulders. Rainbows reflected in the soaring mist of the bright yellow sunlight.

Mr. Ob was sitting cross-legged on a sun-lit black boulder to one side of the waterfall where the mist did not reach, with his arms outstretched, and his face raised to absorb the gentle sunlight. Sensing my presence, he lowered his head and arms and smiled. He motioned to me to sit on a rock near him.

"Nice illusion of the waterfall," Mr. Ob observed, You seem to be getting the hang of making Earth illusions. What have you learned that is of special interest about Earthlings?"

"Many things of amazement," I replied. "In what they consider the present, there is an astonishing diversity of indigenous peoples. There are some who roam jungles, hunting and gathering. There are others who live in cities, crowded, competing against each other for space and ownership of objects and esthetic experiences."

"That seems to happen on most planets where the inhabitants have bodies," Mr. Ob interjected.

"I also noticed that all the populations indulge in tribal activities. As I scanned through time with my Knowledge Plate, I saw groups evolve from small informal tribes to larger tribes with leaders or kings, and then to nations."

"Yes, said Mr. Ob. "Earthling tribes are bound together by shared judgments that their tribe is somehow better than another tribe. They fight wars over whose tribal god or prophet is legitimate. Something called Universities provide tribal membership valued by the victories of sports teams."

I continued, "The nation that Raven and Dave reside in is governed by two warring tribes, each consumed with the idea of preventing the other tribe from winning at anything."

Mr. Ob nodded his head and smiled in agreement. He then said, "Earthlings seem to have a basic need to identify with a tribe. They gather by tens-of-thousands in sports arenas to watch tribal representatives compete."

I added, "I saw in my Knowledge Plate where the 356 Galaxy Governing Board had to intercede to keep a tribe from destroying all life on the planet. They did this in a place they called Atlantis. They also eliminated whole races who made brutal human sacrifices to their gods, and were destined to destroy the tropical rainforest and the global ecology.

Mr. Ob continued, "What have you learned about your subject pair, Raven and Dave?"

"They believe that time and space are not an illusion," I said. "They use measures of the illusions. One of their measures is feet, based on their anatomy, and another is years which relates to their planetary motion."

"I'm familiar with their ideas of measures," commented Mr. Ob.

"The unit Raven is what they call five-and-a-half feet in length. Her body is identified as twenty-eight years old. The protein strings on her head are described as black. She considers the circumference of parts of her body of great importance.

"She worked in something called a school where they read or are told about things. This schooling is very different from our way of learning by having life experiences and observing experiences of those in other space-times. They study only their own history and knowledge base."

Mr. Ob asked, "What life lessons do you think Raven is working on?"

I replied, "She is sharing the experience of a strange energy they call love with her mate and is having an experience they call writing a book."

"Yes," said Mr. Ob. "Unlike here, where we can mentally create and experience anything we desire, they create first in words and then read or recite the words to experience the reality."

He continued, "Do you have any ideas on how you may be of service to her in her life experience?"

I thought for a minute and then said, "I might help her with ideas for her book."

Mr. Ob nodded and then asked, "What about the unit called Dave?"

"Dave is measured as five-and-three-quarters feet in length, with a body occupying thirty-two years of time. His protein strings are black. He shares the idea that some measures of the circumference of Ravens's body are important.

"Dave is something they call a lawyer who has no permanent tribal allegiance. He is hired for inter-tribal warfare over money, possessions, permission to engage in some activity, or to punish each other.

"He is a member of a tribe with a belief in the validity of the simple four-dimensional science. He can get very emotional if someone expresses an idea that disagrees with this belief system."

Mr. Ob smiled and nodded his head in agreement. "Earthlings seem to be stuck in a primitive science. Do you think you can give a little guidance to Dave on that subject as part of your Earthlings 1a assignment of learning to communicate?"

"I will have to do it gently," I cautioned. "His beliefs in their limited science are very set. The female unit, Raven, and Dave entered into a pair-bonding relationship they call married. They still have differences in their belief systems. Dave does not believe there are energies and a reality not described in his science."

Mr. Ob said, "I'm satisfied with your progress on making Earth illusions and how you have observed the pair. You may begin to contact them.

CHAPTER 3

Meet Mason

Ravi hummed as she came out through the screen door, barefoot. Dressed in shorts and a white tank top, carrying two goblets of wine, she flipped her head to get her long black hair away from her eyes, bent down, beamed at Dave with her bright blue eyes and gave him a big kiss.

She is radiant, thought Dave.

She stood and said, "I love the desert! I love our married life!

Dave looked at her in surprise. "I'm glad you like it out here. What brought this on?"

"Oh, I was thinking about a year ago, teaching at Beverly Hills High School."

"Don't you miss your students?" asked Dave.

"Teaching the bright ones was always a delight," answered Ravi.

Dave thought a second and then recalled, "I remember you complaining about the self-importance of the pampered foreign students and their parents."

"That's true," Ravi replied. "They often treated me as though I was one of their maids or a nanny. I hated to have to go through layers of male secretaries and personal assistants to arrange conferences with parents."

Dave observed, "You did have actual princes of middle eastern kingdoms in your classes sometimes."

Ravi wrinkled her nose.

"Do you ever miss being a patent attorney?" she asked.

"You mean driving to work every day in L.A. traffic and arguing with devious people?" said Dave with a frown. No, I love running the Colson Foundation and talking with scientists and mathematicians on a logical basis. Everything is very orderly. No, I don't miss patent work."

"I'm glad,' said Ravi. "And, I'm thankful to your great uncle who willed you this place last fall."

"It's been a great place to start married life," added Dave.

Dave leaned back a bit, looked in her eyes and said, "It is convenient that Colson doesn't care where we live as long as it is near an airport where he can land his Learjet. It's great that we can go back to our Playa Vista condo when we need to cool off, enjoy a bit of urban life or visit a good restaurant."

She kissed him again and said, "Speaking of restaurants, it's almost dinner time."

Dave replied, "Do you want to drive down the hill to the Crystal Sky Country Club for dinner? Or, we could drive into Palmdale–it is only a half hour away."

She stared at Dave a half second and said, "No, I need space. I'll pack a light picnic dinner, and we can hike up the hill to that rock outcropping and find a place with a magnificent view. There is not a bit of wind–which is unusual for here. Let's make the most of it."

"Great!" Dave replied. "We'll need to get back down before dark. I like to see what I'm stepping on or in.

✻✻✻✻✻✻✻

They walked up the hill from their cottage, past the hot tub, along a desert sand pathway. Ravi went first, intent on stopping to examine the plants along the trail, reciting the name of each, and feeling the leaves and branches. Dave followed, carrying their dinner in a pack, admiring the ballet of Ravi's backside.

A rabbit sprang from its hiding place and bounded in zig-zags down the hill.

Ravi said, "Look! There goes an Antelope Jack Rabbit. Look at his big ears! I saw coyote tracks and scat back there. Run rabbit!"

Ravi turned onto a dirt road: a barren strip bulldozed in the raw desert, going up the ridge of the hill. Dave moved to walk alongside her.

"Where does this go?" asked Ravi.

"Nowhere. It's a fire road made to allow trucks and crews to get up the mountain to fight wildfires."

Ravi thought for a while and then said, "Maybe that's an idea for my book. A road to nowhere, just in case someone needs to use it."

Dave didn't comment.

About a half mile up the road they came to a yellow sand and gravel trail leading to a prominent outcropping of fractured sandstone layers pointing diagonally to the sky. Opportunistic clumps of small shrubs and bushes grew in the cracks.

Ravi said, "This is a perfect place. That flat rock can be our table."

Dave took off the pack, placed it on the rock and pulled out two water bottles.

11

They sat down and silently sipped from the water bottles taking in the view of the faint blue outline of the southern Sierras ninety miles across the Mojave Desert to the north, the seemingly endless desert to the east, with hazy red hills and buttes punctuating the landscape.

"Isn't this great? Look at the view! Feel that gentle breeze! Smell the sage!" gushed Ravi as she unzipped the pack, revealing plates, wine glasses, and silverware, all neatly tucked into velcro-closed compartments. She spread a red and white checkered tablecloth on the rock, set out two blue plastic plates and silverware, and produced two crystal flutes that she filled with wine from the bottle in the side pocket of the pack. As a final touch, she placed a cut crystal vase in the center and produced a cluster of daisies from a bag in the cooler pocket.

"It's amazing. When you walk on the desert floor, you hardly notice those little yellow flowers that spring up after even a small rain. From up here, it looks like a carpet of yellow."

Dave was struck by how beautiful Ravi looked, wearing no makeup, glowing with some inner exuberance. Dave saw a golden yellow glow around her face and felt a soft vibration while he looked at her. He felt an energy on his chest, right above his heart.

"We picked a perfect evening," she said softly.

They ate silently, gazing, watching the desert fade.

After they had finished eating, Ravi dug two brandy snifters from the pack, poured from a flask, and said, "To protect us from the desert cold as the sun goes down."

They toasted each other and started to sip, and then they heard: "Greetings this evening as you know time to exist."

Dave looked at a wide-eyed Ravi, who looked shocked.

"Did you hear that?" she asked.

"Yes!" Dave stood up with his fists clenched, in a boxer's stance and said, "Who are you? Show yourself." He picked up a large stone from the ground to use as a weapon.

"Over here," the voice said. "The speck of light. No need for alarm, I come in love and peace."

A few yards away, a broken clear glass bottle was lying at the base of a boulder, an old canning jar from the days when people canned their food. It was among broken brown bottles left after target practice. Inside the bottle was an intense, bright speck of light, like the spot a welder makes when he is arc welding two pieces of metal.

Still shocked, it took Dave a few moments to respond. Dave looked at Ravi, who was now staring at the shards of glass, clutching her brandy snifter to her chest.

Dave thought, *That spot of light could be the laser beam of a gunsight.* "Duck!" he shouted as he pulled Ravi behind the rock to shield her.

"No need for alarm. I come in love and peace," repeated the voice.

They peeked over the rock and looked at the spark.

"Lets run!" Dave whispered to Ravi tugging on her arm.

"No," she replied. "Don't you feel the vibration of peace and love?"

Dave thought, *Oh no, here she goes again with her airy-fairy metaphysical stuff.*

"This could be life-threatening," Dave said in a louder whisper.

Ravi stood up. Dave pulled her down saying, "Are you crazy?"

Ravi stood up again, shaking his grip off and said softly, "Who and where are you?"

"Over here, the spark of light!" the voice replied.

Dave was going to pull her down behind the rock again until he saw the serene look on her face. As she walked toward the spark, he joined her, intent on her protection.

"Come over and sit by me. Let's have a conversation," said the voice.

Ravi sat down. Dave too felt a sense of peace. He wondered if the feeling came from Ravi.

"I apologize for what you call startling you," said the speck of light as it shimmered.

Dave walked over and tentatively touched the broken jar with his finger. It was neither hot nor cold. He picked it up and looked for wires and looked around the boulder for a hidden speaker.

"Bring it over here by me. Put it on the ground so I can look at it," said Ravi.

Dave examined the broken jar and saw the brilliant blue light was coming from a minute spot in the glass. He placed it in front of Ravi, who was sitting cross-legged in a Yoga position. She was in total acceptance of the apparition.

"Let us start over," Dave said with force. "Who and what are you?"

The speck of light shimmered. "I'm communicating with you from another place outside of space-time that you do not yet understand. I come as a friend to have a conversation with you."

"A conversation?" Ravi asked. "How can we hear you? Are you a ghost or an angel or something?"

The speck of light replied, "I'm not a ghost of someone who lived on your planet. An angel is almost the right idea. However, in your civilization you have pictured angels as incarnated into bodies with wings and halos and draped them with flowing robes. I don't have a body to hang wings on. You have also made angels employees of your various, shall we say, tribal gods. Think of me as a freelancer."

"Freelancer? Are you some sort of bounty hunter? Dave asked.

Ravi blurted, "Are we going to abducted?

"No." The light blinked. "I come in love and peace to communicate with you."

"What do we call you?" Ravi asked.

The spark of light replied, "We don't have a name as you think of them where I exist. I perceive that there is some of what you call writing on the glass object. What is it?"

Ravi picked up the broken glass jar and looked at the top. She read aloud the word, "Mason."

The spark replied. "Then, you may address me as 'Mason.'"

"Okay Mason, but where are you?" Ravi asked.

"I have a very different view of reality than that of Earthlings. I'm outside space-time as you know it. Perhaps we can discuss that later."

"You say 'Earthlings.' Does that mean you're from another planet?"

"No, where I live we think of 'Earthlings' as a viewpoint, not as a place. I come from what you might call a state of mind."

Dave wanted to say to Ravi, *run, call 911 or something*. He thought, *This must be a dream or a hallucination. There is no scientific explanation for this. Am I losing it?*

"Why are you talking to us?" Dave inquired as an attempt to bring some logic into the situation.

"I want to learn about you, to find out about life on your planet, become your friend."

"Are you some kind of Genie? Ravi asked. "If I rub the glass will I get wishes?"

"No," said Mason. "I cannot perform what you call magic."

"Okay, but I'm confused," Dave mumbled, thinking *I should get Ravi out of here.* "How do we know we can trust you?"

Mason replied, "How much damage can a spark of light do? I've no physical presence on Earth. I'm not visiting in a spaceship that can beam you up. I'm not here in what you call physically. I'm here only as information, such as might occur if you were talking on a telephone. However, if you do not wish to communicate with me, I will disappear from your lives."

"No!" Ravi blurted. "You seem okay. I'm writing a book and maybe I can get some new ideas from you." She looked at Dave with a serene smile. "Okay?"

Before Dave could answer, Mason interrupted and said, "I will go now, and let you, as you say, think about it. If you decide we should communicate, I will return."

The speck of bright light disappeared. Ravi picked up the broken bottle and peered at where the spark had been. "It just looks like an old desert-dirty piece of glass. Was that brandy drugged?"

"I think it must have been or something like that," Dave replied. "There must be a rational scientific explanation for this. Let's pack up and get the hell out of here."

As Ravi was putting everything back into the pack, she walked over and picked up the piece of glass. She looked at Dave with a questioning expression.

Dave shrugged his shoulders and said, "Okay."

She wrapped it in the tablecloth and put it in the pack.

They walked down the fire road holding hands, mulling the recent event over in their minds. Dave followed Ravi as she turned down the trail to their house.

"We've some wine and brandy left. Let's stop at the hot tub," Dave said. "I need to think–or not think."

Dusk faded to dark, the stars came out, the hot tub steamed, a coyote howled, and thoughts of aliens dissolved.

The next morning, after breakfast, Dave was sitting on the porch finishing his second cup of coffee, thinking about their previous night's encounter. *Our experience last night was unscientific. There is no physical way we could be receiving messages from some source light-years away. There is no scientific explanation. It must be some elaborate illusion being created by some prankster. Maybe some disgruntled employee at the winery put a hallucinogenic compound in that bottle. I wonder if I ought to send the bottle to be analyzed. Should I turn this into a lawsuit?*

Ravi came out carrying the broken piece of glass on a folded towel like a ring bearer in a wedding. She was staring at it intensely.

"What should we do with it? Should we build a little shrine or something to place it in?" she asked.

Dave replied, "Well, last night in the hot tub, we decided I would have no part in this. You can talk to the jar or not. Put the damn thing over there in the corner under the extra chair."

Ravi placed the glass under the chair and then stared at Dave a long time. "What's going on? You have gone away again. You have retreated into that emotional fortification of yours. You are 'all castle' and 'no drawbridge' again. Open up, I'm here, your wife. Remember? Out here in the meadow with the flowers. Let me in!"

Dave replied, "I'm sorry. Even though we talked about it last night, I have trouble with the idea of aliens from other planets talking to me. It goes against the grain of my scientific education. I don't know why it upsets me."

"Well, get over it. I'm tired of this. Every time I broach a metaphysical idea, you withdraw into that emotional fortification, and pull up the drawbridge."

She walked over, sat down on his lap, kissed him lightly, and said, "You're under siege! I'm not leaving until you come out and surrender. Fire the trebuchet!"

She gave him a big wet kiss.

"Take that!"

"I surrender?" Dave asked meekly.

She kissed him again for a long time, looked into his eyes, and said, "Okay, you're back."

She stood and said,"I want to talk about Mason. What's your problem?"

"I love our life! I'd prefer things to stay just the way they are," Dave replied.We've had a lot of change in our lives this past year. I'd like to keep things as they are."

"How do you think talking to a piece of broken glass is going to change our lives?" asked Ravi.

"As we talked about last night, there is absolutely no logical or scientific explanation for a voice coming out of a piece of broken glass. I'm a scientific person. I'd have to change who I am to talk to a piece of glass."

Ravi and Dave stared at the jar for a while, but nothing happened.

Dave pulled Ravi onto his lap and said, "I love you."

"I love you too! Ravi smiled and purred, "Now kiss me."

They didn't notice the brief flash of light in the jar. Mason thought, *What is that unusual energy? We do not have that in our reality*

CHAPTER 4

Ravi Sees a UFO

The next day, after breakfast, Ravi and Dave were enjoying their usual morning activity of sitting on the front porch, gazing across the Mojave desert to the north, quietly sipping coffee. The air was crystal clear, and they could see the southern end of the Sierra Nevada mountain range, ninety miles away.

"What is that flying way out there?" asked Ravi.

"I don't see anything. The Palmdale Airport where they build and test spy planes and drones is in that direction. Farther out is Edwards Air Force Base where the Space Shuttles used to land. There is no telling what kind of flying object you can see out there."

"I think it was a UFO! It didn't move like an airplane. It was there and then it disappeared."

Dave thought for a second. "We get a lot of mirage effects in the desert where things can appear and then disappear."

Ravi picked up her iPad from the table. "I'm searching 'Edwards Air Force base unidentified flying object' to see if they have UFO sightings." She read for a minute and then continued, "Look, there are pages and pages of references."

She read, "On May 16, 1965, at about 1:30 or so in the morning, the Air Traffic Controller on duty in the tower saw objects in the sky that appeared on the base radars, and were seen by many people. They even scrambled a jet to intercept them. The incident apparently went on until daybreak. Most of the other website search hits seem to be referencing the same event. They seem to be UFO and conspiracy-oriented.

Dave assumed his lawyerly demeanor reserved for cross-examination and said, "What is the source of that report?" While thinking, *There is no credible scientific evidence to support UFO sightings.*

She studied for a minute. "The website says the report is from official government sources."

Dave continued with his lawyerly demeanor. "And what organization owns the website?"

"It says it's an organization devoted to researching the truth about UFOs."

Dave smirked and retorted. "Do you think that they are necessarily an unbiassed source?"

Ravi shrank down in her chair a little and then said, "I guess you're right."

She read some more. "There doesn't seem to be many UFO sightings reported recently."

"There is a logical explanation for that." Dave offered. "In 1965, we were in the middle of the Cold War. People were pretty paranoid then. Search for 'UFO Project Blue Book.'"

In a minute, Ravi waved her iPad "Here it is, from the National Archives. How is that for a reliable source? It shows the searches done under the Freedom of Information Act for Project Blue Book. It says the Air Force studied all the reported sightings from 1947 until 1969 when they closed the project. The Air Force concluded that:

(1) no UFO reported, investigated, and evaluated by the Air Force has ever given any indication of threat to our national security;

(2) there has been no evidence submitted to or discovered by the Air Force that sightings categorized as "unidentified" represent technological developments or principles beyond the range of present-day scientific knowledge; and

(3) there has been no evidence indicating that sightings categorized as "unidentified" are extraterrestrial vehicles.'

"I guess they decided that there was no such thing as UFOs, she added meekly."

Dave delighted in scoring his points, "It was at a time when they were spending incredible amounts of money on fighter jets, bombers, and anti-aircraft and intercontinental ballistic missiles."

"During what they called *The Cold War?*" asked Ravi.

"Yes, It was a crazy time. Can you imagine the plight of the poor Air Force officer assigned to Project Blue Book? What would happen to the poor officer if he came forward and announced, 'We have proof that flying saucers move at will over our country observing our military installations. We have no idea of who or what they are. We have no aircraft or missiles capable of intercepting them. We are completely vulnerable.'"

"He would get more attention than he wanted," observed Ravi.

Dave continued, "Think of the congressional hearing circus that would follow and all the Generals whose careers would be tarnished by admitting the military was impotent against UFOs.

"From a career standpoint, the Blue Book officer only had one option: hypothesize that there is no such thing as UFOs. He could hire a consultant who would go through the data and prove the hypothesis using scientific methods."

Ravi read a little more and then said, "The Air Force decided that they didn't have a budget for keeping track of UFO sightings. They stated:

'There are a number of universities and professional scientific organizations . . . and private organizations interested in aerial phenomena . . . to ensure that sound evidence will not be overlooked by the scientific community.'"

Dave chided, "That is a clever trick. Turn the job over to conspiracy theorists, kooks, and cranks, then let them go crazy and discredit the whole idea."

Ravi shook her head. "I guess I didn't see a UFO." She studied him and then said, "You're gone again. Tell the Lord of Scientific Truth to let down the damned drawbridge to his castle and come back out here or else he can sleep in the desert with the rattlesnakes tonight."

Dave slumped in his chair and said, "Okay, you caught me. I apologize for getting on my high horse and defending my client, scientific truth. I still have problems with talking about things that are outside of the realms of science.

"I don't want to spend the night sleeping under a Joshua tree with rattlesnakes. Changing the subject, how is the great American novel coming? Are you ever going to tell me about it?"

"No," said Ravi, "I'm still struggling to get a story. Maybe I should have UFOs in my novel."

Dave scowled. "I think I need to go for a run and get this out of my system."

"Please do," replied Ravi with a scowl that matched his. "Run a long way in a straight line away from here."

An hour later, Dave returned.

Ravi was sitting on porch intently keying something in on her laptop. She didn't look up.

Dave sheepishly looked at Ravi. "I'm sorry for turning into the arrogant scientist against you."

Ravi looked up and said, "Apology accepted. Now go get in the shower. She stood up, started unbuttoning her blouse, and said, "I'll join you in a minute. We need to talk."

CHAPTER 5

Wrong Number

That evening, the desert air was calm as the sun faded behind the hills, leaving an aquatic blue and red sky celebrating the end of the day. Dave sat on the porch reading from his iPad. Ravi hummed as she butted the screen door open and twirled outside with a can of Coors, a glass of wine, and a crystal tray of olives, celery, and chopped vegetables.

"Time to knock off," she said, handing Dave the can of beer. "Look at that sunset! When there is no wind, they dazzle. Look! Over there!" She pointed north toward the Sierras. "I think I saw another UFO! That's the direction of Edwards Air Force Base."

Dave was puzzled and said, "I saw a flash too. They now call the facility the Air Force Test Center. We probably saw a glint from some classified airplane."

Ravi looked excited. "I'd like to find out what they do up there. She took the iPad from Dave and typed. After a minute she said, "Wikipedia has a history of the center. It says they give tours of the Test Center Museum. Let's go sometime. I wonder if it has UFO stuff? The page shows their number."

She picked up her iPhone, and using her stylus, tapped in the number, then listened while it rang seven times. Finally, a male voice answered and said, "Hello."

Ravi said, "What hours and days is the museum open? I'd like to examine UFO files."

There was a long pause, and the male voice said, "Lady, you have the wrong number," and hung up.

Ravi looked at her iPhone and then the page on the iPad and said, "Oh, I called the wrong number." She tried again and listened for a few seconds, then reported, "A recording announced that they've stopped giving tours of the museum for budgetary reasons."

CHAPTER 6

Duty Officer Notes

In an unmarked building, dating from the 1960s, located in a warehouse area of the Air Force Test Center, the Duty Officer logged Ravi's call into the database. From the caller ID, he got her name and address. He listened to the recording of Ravi's question and typed in her exact words. He hit decode and looked at the answer that blinked red on his screen. He checked Ravi's recording with his transcription. They agreed. He did a manual check. "What hours and days is the museum open? I'd like to examine UFO files" 4 (the number of letters in the first word), 5 (the number of letters in the second word), 3,4,2,3,6,4,2,4,2,7,3,5.

He manually entered 4534-2364-24-2735. The computer blinked red with "Code 547 Red Alert." He clicked on the red button that said EXECUTE.

Phones rang. Alarms sounded. Gates closed. Men in gray uniforms donned body armor and scrambled. Hangar doors glided closed as klaxons blared. Desert camouflage-painted armored vehicles deployed into the quiet of the evening.

CHAPTER 7

Meeting with Colson

Ravi was sitting on the deck staring across the desert, thinking about her novel. Dave walked out through the screen door. He looked a little concerned as he said, "Vince texted me that he wants to meet us for lunch today at the Palmdale Regional Airport terminal. He specifically requested that you come along. I wonder what this is all about."

Ravi looked puzzled and replied, "I didn't even know there was a Palmdale Regional Airport terminal."

Dave frowned as he said, "Vince gave me instructions how to get there. It's closed. The city of Palmdale built an airport terminal, but few people wanted to fly in or out of there. Commercial flights stopped years ago."

"Is that the same as the Palmdale Airport?" asked Ravi.

"Yes, they shared the same runway. The Regional Airport Terminal sits alone on this side. Colson said to meet at the end of the taxi way, east of the terminal. I looked at the satellite photos on Google, and the terminal is abandoned."

Ravi's eyes grew wide. "Where will we have lunch? I doubt if there are any four-star restaurants in the middle of the desert. It doesn't sound like Vince's usual choice of dining."

"No. This meeting is about something else, something too confidential to talk about on the phone or email. It must be something he thinks is important if he is traveling down here from his Palo Alto office."

Ravi smiled and said, "I'll get to wear a dress! I haven't had an occasion for weeks. How about the white one with the orange flowers? Or, should I dress in something more businesslike for lunch with your boss?"

"The white one will be fine. Meeting at an abandoned airport in the middle of the Mojave Desert can't be too formal."

✻ ✻ ✻ ✻ ✻ ✻

It was a comfortable seventy degrees as they drove with the Porsche top down across the barren desert toward Palmdale.

"There are still a few desert wildflowers along the side of the road," observed Ravi. "I like going this back way into Palmdale. Oh look! Up there! A UFO!"

Dave glanced up and said, "No, that is a military drone aircraft."

Ravi looked wide-eyed and asked, "Like in Afghanistan? Is it looking at us? Are we in its gunsights? Is there something in your background you haven't told me? Look. It's circling!" She slid down in her seat and pulled her ball cap down over her eyes to hide.

Dave laughed and said, "Relax. There are several experimental drone flight test fields out here. During World War II, the army built training airports here, far from civilization. They were abandoned to the desert until a few years ago when the military drone makers bought them for testing. See that gray hill over there? That's called Grey Butte. One of the old World War II airports is there. It has been rehydrated into a test field for drones.

Ravi peeked out from under her hat and implored, "Can't we go a little faster?"

Dave was silent for about a minute while he kept one eye on the drone and then said, "I do think it is circling and following us."

❄ ❄ ❄ ❄ ❄ ❄

In a camouflage-painted van at Grey Butte Field, two young men were staring intently at their drone control consoles.

"She's hot! We don't get many of them out here," said the first technician.

"Use high resolution. See if you can get the license plate."

"There I got it," said the second tech.

"See if we can look down the top of her dress. Hey! That's good. I love these new high res optics. Look! Her dress blew up her legs.

"Okay, let's begin the test of the auto track program with this target of opportunity."

"I wonder who the dude driving the car is? Let's test the vehicle ID software."

❄ ❄ ❄ ❄ ❄ ❄

"Are we almost there yet? Ravi asked, still scrunching down in her seat."

"Only a couple of miles now. I think our companion left. You can come out now. He did seem to be following us. Kind of spooky when we are going to what appears to be a clandestine meeting with Colson."

Ravi emerged and looked around. "Maybe it has some sort of invisibility cloak. Are you sure it is gone?"

Dave made a turn and said, "There, you can see Palmdale Regional Airport, in all its glory in the distance."

As they neared the airport Ravi said, "The whole parking area is empty. Are you sure this is it? What time is it?"

"Almost twelve. We're five minutes early. Down at the end of the taxiway there is a white thing. That's where we're supposed to meet."

As they got nearer, they could see that the white thing was a catering truck near a pavilion that had been set up. A black sedan was parked behind the truck, apparently belonging to the muscular man, obviously a weightlifter, in a white polo shirt, wearing dark aviator sunglasses, and black pants, standing in the shade of the truck.

A man in a chef's hat working at the truck waved to them as they neared. They parked and were greeted the chef carrying a tray of iced tea and water.

"Welcome, Mr. Willard. Right on time," he said, pointing in the distance as a Learjet touched down near the end of the runway.

They drank iced tea until the jet taxied up and stopped a hundred feet away. The door opened, and Vince Colson, dressed in a white sports shirt, khaki slacks, and black leather-topped running shoes climbed down. The pilot followed and handed Vince his brief case.

He walked over to Dave. With a broad smile, he extended his hand and said, "How good to see you again. I like the work you've been doing for us. Your last report on the foundation showed it's headed in exactly the right direction." He then turned to Ravi and said, "Raven, you are looking radiant. This desert life agrees with you. Let's sit down and enjoy lunch."

He motioned to the table under the white pavilion, set for three, with a white tablecloth, bright blue stoneware plates, and red cloth napkins.

Dave noticed that the pilot and copilot of the Learjet were seated at another table near the catering truck. White polo shirt stood, alert.

Vince began, "It's very convenient that you live out here and we can get together for lunch so painlessly. Our pilots much prefer landing here rather than threading their way into LAX. It's easier to have the restaurant come to us than fighting the L.A. traffic. We've had meetings here before when I had business with some people who work on the other side of the field. It's a nice private spot."

The man in the chef's hat appeared and took their drink orders. White polo shirt watched attentively.

Ravi volunteered, "Is this place private enough to get together? One of those drone airplanes followed us as we drove here. It was creepy."

Dave was quick to respond. "The people who make and test military drones use some of the nearby abandoned World War II airports as flight test bases."

Vince smiled and said, "I don't think any drones can eavesdrop on our conversations yet. Raven, I imagine you should be accustomed to being looked at."

After more small talk, and the main course, Vince began, "Last week I flew to London. As usual, traffic was backed up going into Heathrow, and we had to circle in a holding pattern for about a half hour. We saw something interesting that I would like to have you check out for us. I'll let our pilot Stephanie tell you about it."

He waved to the pilots sitting at the other table and the tall, slender pilot, about thirty years old, in black pants and white blouse with epaulettes, hurried over.

"Stephanie, tell our guests what we saw while holding for Heathrow."

She began, "Air traffic control put us in an elliptical holding pattern about a hundred miles west of LHR. Because of our size, they put us in a low stack. Bob, my copilot, and I always try to make a game out of holding patterns by flying precision patterns that go exactly over the same landmark on each pass around the ellipse. This time, we picked an obelisk, some kind of war monument, near a large chalk horse figure carved in a hill. We were observing the area closely on our first pass. On the second pass, clouds obscured our view. On the third pass, we saw something that was not there on our first pass. In a field below the horse, a large geometric figure had been carved in the wheat crop. Here, I have a photo of it."

She pulled her iPhone out of her pocket, thumbed to the picture, and handed it to Dave. He looked at it for a second, holding it so Ravi could also see.

Dave offered it to Vince, but he shook his head and said, "I saw it. On our fourth pass around the pattern, Stephanie pointed it out to us."

As Dave handed back her phone, Vince said to Stephanie, "Stephanie, thanks. I didn't know you had a picture."

Stephanie tipped her cap, nodded to everyone and walked back to her table.

Vince added, "Of course, that was a crop circle, today's version. Have you heard of them?"

Assuming his straight-backed lawyer posture, Dave replied, "I read about them years ago. I thought they were exposed as fakes when locals bragged in a pub that they had been making them as a joke. I remember they had caused quite a stir before their fraud was exposed. I thought that ended the interest in the circles."

Vince nodded his head in agreement and then added, "That's what I remembered too. But, on that trip to London, I had lunch with an old friend of mine in the Ministry of Defense. He changed the subject when I mentioned to him about seeing the circle. My intuition told me it was something he couldn't talk about. He also mentioned that ball lightning has been seen near crop circles."

Ravi frowned and looked puzzled, so Vince continued, "Since the middle ages, some people near lightning storms have seen basketball-sized spheres of bright glowing light floating a few feet above the ground. Many sightings were documented by famous writers of the time.

"I'm considering a large investment," Vince continued, "in a company doing research in high-energy fields and plasmas. I'd like you to set aside other foundation business for awhile and investigate this for me. If there are potential patents or trade secrets involved in ball lightning and crop circles, I need to know."

Oh no! Dave thought, *More of this paranormal stuff. I can hardly wait to interview all the kooks that are involved.*

"Vince," he answered, "I can interrupt the grant processing I've been doing. Sounds intriguing. Have you got a starting point?"

Vince, replied, "I've been doing some online research. You're going to have to get past a lot of metaphysical ideas to get to the science if you investigate crop circles. I think you're going to need some left-brain help with that."

He turned to Ravi and said, "Could you be available to help Dave with this as an employee of the foundation? There will be some hardships, of course. You will have to travel with and assist him with his research in England."

Ravi looked stunned and then said, "I guess so."

"Dave, is this all right with you? Vince asked. "I know you must hate to give up extended traveling alone and dining by yourself."

Dave's bewilderment vanished, and he said with a smile, "Oh, I think I could accommodate that."

"Then, Dave, draw up a contract. Double the salary she made as a teacher."

Dave nodded in agreement.

Vince turned to Ravi and said, "You'll need a title. How about 'Associate Director of The Colson Foundation?'"

Ravi blushed, smiled meekly, and said, "That's fine."

Vince reached into his briefcase and pulled out a box of business cards, and handed them to Ravi. "I took the liberty of having business cards made for you. Is everything on them okay?"

Ravi stared at them with her mouth open in surprise and said, "Yes, everything's correct. Do we use the foundation's Palo Alto address?"

"Dave wanted it," Vince replied, "since he decided not to open an office in LA. Nearly all of our correspondence is via the internet these days, so it's not a problem."

Vince reached across the table, shook her hand and said, "Welcome aboard."

He turned to Dave and said, "Back to your question: After you read up on crop circles, go to England and check them out. Talk to locals and scientists that may have been involved.

He looked at his watch and said, "Regrettably, it's time to go to another meeting. Welcome aboard Raven." He shook their hands as he got up.

They watched as Vince boarded the plane and it then taxied away.

White polo shirt stood with his hands folded in front of him until Vince's plane was airborne and then drove off in his black sedan.

Dave and Ravi got back in the Porsche and started home. Ravi stared at her business cards.

Dave thought, "*Dealing with kooks who had unscientific beliefs is never fun. I'll love having her along, but we're going to create some conflicts.*

After a while Ravi said, "Dammit, there you go again. Let down the drawbridge."

Dave replied, "I'm sorry. I still find it difficult to deal with all this metaphysical stuff. It is against my scientific training." He thought, *Crop circles are probably all hogwash!*

As they drove they discussed their plans, as the Director and the Associate Director.

Dave saw the drone following them again, but he didn't say anything.

Chapter 8

My Next Assignment

My next meeting with Mr. Ob required some climbing, which I created as a way to enjoy some beautiful Earth scenery. As I started, I walked through a meadow with brilliant yellow sunflowers turning to greet the early morning sunlight as bees buzzed doing their bee jobs. The trail zig-zagged up the hill through scrub brush, passing a small stand of flowering fruit trees to a meadow. The meadow ended at a cliff overlooking the valley of our campus. There, Mr. Ob was standing on the edge, arms outstretched, eyes closed. His white robe blew in the gentle wind. He sensed me and turned, smiling.

"How delightful to see you," he said. You are accomplishing your assignment of creating earth realities very well. This creation is a nice place to meet. Those are great clouds in the distance over the valley. You create that sort of detail well."

We sat down on the fresh spring grass, and Mr. Ob asked, "How are you doing on your contacts?"

"I've now communicated with both members of the pair. Their intense energy field when they are together is quite interesting. The male has a reactive response whenever somebody says something that conflicts with his belief system. He stops all energy outflows and surrounds himself with a dense, energetic barrier."

"That is common," Mr. Ob replied. "It's quite a contrast to our reality that is based on connections. Many Earthlings surround themselves with a barrier to isolate and protect themselves from others. However, it only serves to prevent them from learning and having new experiences. You and I perceive energetic flows from Earthling bodies. "However, the human species seems to ignore them and communicates with something we don't have which they call emotions."

Mr. Ob took my Knowledge Plate and held it so both of our hands were on the sides. "Direct me to your space-time bookmarks in the plate when the pair did something you found of interest."

Mr. Ob observed for a while. "That's good. You have marked incidents in the lives of his pair that allow us to know what their beliefs and activities are. Keep up communication with them. You may proceed on to your middle school science experiment. Have you thought about what you would like to do?"

I thought for a minute and then said, "A friend of mine said that, for his Earthlings 1a middle school science project, he produced translucent apparitions in that vaguely resembled human bodies. He would make them appear before Earthlings in different situations and then observe the Earthlings' responses. Although the apparitions were nothing more than images, Earthlings identified the apparitions as many things such as departed dead souls, demons, or tribal gods. Sometimes they assigned great power or wisdom to the images. He said that some Earthlings believed that these apparitions gave them messages, and assumed positions of tribal authority because they had special knowledge. My friend had many interesting stories of how creation of a simple apparition could lead to amazing responses."

"They are a delightful species. What experiment would you like to do?" replied Mr. Ob.

"I'd like to produce some minor physical effect at different times through what they call history and see how they respond."

Mr. Ob looked delighted as he said, "An old friend of mine who is working in the Eight-dimensional Travel Laboratory has recently started developing apparatus that might be useful to you. He likes to invent stuff and is delighted to find someone who can use it in an experiment. I'll ask him if he would like to work with you."

Mr. Ob paused for a while with his eyes closed and then said, "His name is Dr. Ev. I explained to him what you want to do, and he said he had a new invention he would be delighted for you to try out. He can see you now."

I should explain about that form of communication. In our reality, we do not use devices like your cell phones to communicate. We tune our consciousness to another person, and we are immediately "talking" to them. While Mr. Ob had his eyes closed, he had a conversation with Dr. Ev.

Mr. Ob said, "The Eight-dimensional Travel Laboratory is semi-physical. It's a joint creation of many people, held in place by an agreement of that group consciousness. Your Knowledge Plate can guide you into entering into the agreement of that reality.

"Dr. Ev has arranged for a tour of Earth so you can get a better feel for the place before you design your experiment. Let me know when you and Dr. Ev have decided on an experiment. I'll guide you to the laboratory now."

I experience a momentary flash of dull light, like being in a dense fog.

Chapter 9

Mason Reappears

As they drove into the carport of their desert home, Ravi said, "I'm excited about this. I get to do real research, not like writing a comparison of the ideas of Milton and Arthur C. Clarke that few will ever read. This investigation is something going on with real people!"

She sprang from the car, ran into the living room, picked up her laptop, rushed to the front deck and began to type.

Dave followed and said, "Would you like something to drink? Water, iced tea?"

"No, thanks. I'll get something in a little while."

Dave sat down and mused, *Why is this happening? Things were going so good. Now I have to go to England and trudge through cow pastures looking for signs of aliens. At times, I miss digging down into a multiyear drug patent case with a settlement in the hundreds of millions.*

"Look!" Ravi said, "I Googled crop circles and got over four thousand hits. The first one is from New Haven, Connecticut."

Ravi read a while and then said, "That one was about some locals tramping in the snow."

Dave thought, *Fine, we should by all means go to Connecticut and talk to them.*

Ravi continued, "Here is a self-described snow artist who wears snowshoes to make gigantic geometric crop-circle-like patterns. Some cover whole ski hills in the French Alps. It says he's an engineer and likes to do mathematical figures. He spends ten hours to make one. Maybe that is what my novel should be about: a snow artist."

"Now you're talking." Dave said with enthusiasm, "Next winter we'll have to take our skis and go to the French Alps. I think I could get excited about this."

"And look! There are even sand artists raking patterns on beaches that look like crop circles."

"My kind of people, dirt artists," Dave quipped.

"Ah! Here are some sites with British crop circles." She read a while and then said, "They have many ideas about who or what is making crop circles. This page says they're caused by paranormal activity or UFOs."

She stared at Dave for a second and then said, "Stop it! "You are all castle, moat, and no drawbridge again. Don't lock me out. What's going on?"

Dave replied, "I'm sorry. I can't get excited about investigating paranormal phenomena or UFOs. I don't look forward to dealing with a bunch of nary-fairy weirdos. I need something solid for my logical, scientific mind."

Ravi fixed her gaze at him and said, "Being logical and scientific is one thing, withdrawing from me when certain subjects come up is another. Get over it!"

Dave thought for a minute and said, "You're right. I apologize. After I work on this subject more, and see how this is related to the foundation research, I'll get over it."

Ravi turned to her laptop and said, "Why don't you get us something cold to drink while I check on when the most likely time that crop circles happen."

After Dave had returned with two large glasses of ice water, Ravi said, "Surprise! Crop circles only appear when there are crops. The wheat and other crops get tall enough for circles about June. The farmers harvest the wheat in late August. If we're going to see crop circles, it looks like mid-June is the time."

Dave thought a beat and then said, "June is peak travel season. We'd better make travel arrangements. Let's allow about a week there. Go ahead and make airline arrangements to London. We can work out a detailed itinerary after we do some more research."

Ravi bounced up and down in her chair and said, "I like this job."

They both spent the rest of the afternoon reading and learning about crop circles.

Ravi said, "Oh boy, this is exciting!"

Dave thought, *How did I get myself into this?*

"Quitting time! Let's knock off for the day," Ravi said as she closed her laptop. "It's been quite a day. This morning, I was an unemployed writer struggling to think up a story. Then a drone spy plane chased us, we ate a surreal lunch at an abandoned airport; a foundation hired me—I guess that means you're technically my boss—and we're scheduled to leave for England in about a month."

Dave put down his iPad and answered, "I started the day running a foundation sponsoring nice, neat solid mathematical research, and now I'm headed to England to talk to kooks."

He looked at Ravi and added, You're positively beaming with excitement, and that'll be a great adventure to share, no matter how it all turns out."

Ravi smiled, walked over, sat on his lap, gave Dave a big kiss and said, "I love our life!"

❋ ❋ ❋ ❋ ❋ ❋

After dinner, they returned to the deck to enjoy the last of the sunset and the evening. It was still and quiet as the last golden rays of the sun disappeared, and the azure sky faded. They drank herbal tea and listened to the kangaroo rats shake the sage bushes. A coyote greeted the evening. Varmints emerged.

"Look there's the evening star."

"That is Hesperus," Dave explained, "leading the stars into the night, according to the Greeks."

Ravi said, "Yes, I know. He comes from The Garden of the Hesperides where the golden apples grew." She thought for a minute and then said, "Crop circles are kind of like mythology. A lot of interpretation is added to whatever is observed."

Then they heard, "Good evening, as you believe time to exist." A bright blue spark of light flashed from within the broken Mason jar under the chair. "I bring you greetings."

Ravi's eyes grew wide, and she spilled her tea. She looked at Dave and raised her eyebrows as though asking a question.

Dave nodded.

She said, "Mason? We didn't know if you were coming back! Dave decided he'll be concentrating on work. He said it would be okay if I communicated with you."

Mason responded, "I understand why he made that decision. You should understand that you have free will and can decide whether to interact with me at any time, as you believe time to exist.

"Now I know we weren't drugged by some hallucinogen when you introduced yourself up the hill," Dave added.

Mason continued, "I'm delighted that I've been able to inspire that belief."

The blue light blinked, and Mason said, "The purpose of my communication, at this time, is to go over the ideas of space and time and how it is I can be known to you. May we talk about that briefly while I'm here today?"

Dave shrugged his shoulders.

Ravi spoke up, "I love talking to you, even though science isn't my subject. It's my husband who needs to fit our interaction into some physical theory."

Mason replied, "Now, as you believe time to exist, we must discuss the subject you call Physics. With your planetary belief system, reality exists in four dimensions. Information must flow through wires, air, as radio waves, or on laser beams, stuff that is included in your four-dimensional physics. Nothing can travel faster than what you call the speed of light."

"That's what all the scientists I know believe," Dave commented.

"We live in a reality that has your four-dimensions plus four additional dimensions," Mason continued. "In your reality, the distance from San Francisco and Boston is thousands of miles. In eight dimensions, there are shortcuts or folds in space-time producing no separation at all between San Francisco and Boston. Information can flow between the two places without being carried by physical objects, such as a book, or a field such as a radio wave, and can travel by a different set of rules. Thought and your emotional vibrations travel via those shortcuts. If you are in San

Francisco and think about a friend in Boston you can exchange information with them via shortcuts."

Ravi said, "I don't comprehend all that dimensional stuff. Did you have to travel a long way to talk to us?"

"You should understand that I'm not visiting you in what you call a physical sense. You perceive me in the form of information. You have to notice that I don't have a body. I'm communicating with you through one of the shortcut folds in space-time. I'm creating this spark of light as what you might call an illusion."

"Then, you are here only in spirit?" Ravi asked.

Mason replied, "That is almost the right idea."

"I'll have to come back to this idea later after I understand more about space-time physics," said Dave. "How can I find out more about the theory you profess?"

Mason replied, "One minute please, as you believe time to exist, and I will get you an answer."

After only a few seconds, Mason said, "I perceive that a female energy is working on space-time mathematics for you."

"Would that be Candice Montgomery?" Dave inquired.

Mason replied, "As you turned your attention to her, I could sense her vibration. I perceive she has the knowledge you seek. This is enough of physics. Ravi, how is the great American novel coming along?"

"How do you know about that?" Ravi asked.

"We perceive in your vibration the idea of creating what you call a book," said Mason.

"I've lots of ideas for my book but still not a real story in mind."

"A story about tribes might be good. When I scan through what you call your planetary history, that seems to be a dominant idea. We see small nomadic tribes merging into larger tribes, then nations. Nations fight wars over dirt considered tribal property, over grudges between tribal chiefs, and over who follows the true tribal prophet or the real God. We watch in amazement how some tribes, in what you call now, are fighting ancient grudges with modern weapons. There are many stories to be told there."

"Most of the stories of our ancient tribes," Ravi said, "the Greek, Roman, and Egyptian mythology, are full of stories of wars and conquest. Our history texts are about who was conquering who through time. Is your world going to invade ours?"

"No, we come in love and peace. We respect your personal and planetary civilization's journey of learning. On your planet, you have what you call textbooks that teach you lessons from what you call the past. On ours, we learn through studying many planetary civilizations, such as yours, in their various stages of evolution."

Ravi asked, "How many civilizations?"

"In what you would call our schools, we have the opportunity to study over three hundred civilizations," Mason replied. "I've looked at twenty-nine planetary forms of life, some in early stages of development. But this a subject, for what you say, is, for another time."

The blue spark began to fade. "I'll say goodbye. I'm running out of the energy I use to visit you. I have to, as you say, go now, even though space and time are only an illusion. There is no place to go, and the time is only now. If you want to continue this discussion in what you call the future, simply rub this jar and say my name."

The light in the jar went out.

Ravi took Dave's hand and said, "Are you sure it's not going to upset you and cause you to go away if I talk to Mason from time to time?"

Dave replied, "The mystery of who or what is making crop circles is a big enough problem for me to solve right now. I don't want to grapple with the question of how an alien light years away can communicate with us. If you feel okay with talking to Mason, go ahead. Please don't do it when I'm present."

Ravi stared at him for a second and then said, "Okay, mister scientist. You are making progress. Just don't pull up your drawbridge and go away."

"Okay," Dave replied. "I guess I need to abdicate my crown as Lord, Defender of Scientific Truth."

CHAPTER 10

Mason's Earth Tour

I experienced a momentary flash of dull light, like being in a dense fog, and then found myself standing on a grass-covered slope. I created the illusion of having hands protruding from a white robe and then put them on my Knowledge Plate. A gleaming building of silver glass appeared in front of me, several stories high, located on a lake shore, surrounded by trees in golden fall color. At the entrance, I was met by a bald man wearing a blue business suit under a white laboratory jacket with a blue plastic identification tag clipped to the pocket. The tag said Dr. Ev, Project Scientist and had a badge number and a laboratory logo of a figure eight dissolving at the top and bottom.

Dr. Ev said, "Since you are investigating Earthlings, you have come to the right space-time location, the Eight-dimensional Travel Laboratory. The hundreds of individuals involved in this project are jointly creating a laboratory in the form of a place on Earth. It is an illusion of such intensity it is half-way physical. You might say it is like meeting Earth half way. Inside the building, you will pick up what we call a bodysuit to be able to persist in the illusion. Our bodysuits are tailored to look like those created by

Earthlings for illusions they call movies. Here, clip on this visitor's badge."

As I clipped the badge on my flowing robe, there was a flash of light, and I was in a white-walled room filled with glass-doored lockers. In many of the lockers were inanimate gray bodies clothed in a metallic gray garment you Earthlings would call a jumpsuit.

Dr. Ev walked to a locker and opened the door. There was a flash of light, and he morphed into a little gray man. In Earth terms, he was about four feet tall, with a head much larger in proportion to the body, with no hair, and having large elliptical yellow eyes. He had only slits for ears and a small mouth with no lips."

He smiled a little smile, which was all the body-suit could do, and, pointing to another locker, said, "This will be your locker, Come and suit up."

I walked over, opened the door, and saw a blinding flash. I felt strange and looked down and saw that I was now in a gray bodysuit that looked like Dr. Ev's.

"I understand that Mason is the name by which they identify you on Earth. We will refer to you by that name when you are using the body- suit. You will get used to the bodysuit after a while. Let me show you around."

We were in a cavernous building, with floor after floor of open offices, surrounding an atrium with growing trees. An open creek flowed through the center, complete with golden fish. Many bodysuits with identification badges walked, silent. Hundreds of others sat, meditating.

"What are they all doing?" I asked.

Dr. Ev replied, "They are using meditation to create the shared illusion of this building. The illusion of the whole laboratory is too expansive and solid for a single being to create.

"Mr. Oz and I decided that you should start with an Earth tour. The tour vehicles are in the vehicle laboratory over on the right."

We walked through a door into a large cubical room. I saw gray cabinets with blinking lights, coils of pipe, and mazes of wires on the four walls. A dimly-lit glass enclosure contained a gantry enclosing a nest of girders and three gimbals. A small pod was in the center of the gimbals.

"We all have the ability to travel perceptually through space-time instantaneously," Dr. Ev began. "You do this by concentrating on a crystalline object that is near the Earthlings you were assigned to study. With the intelligence of the pod computer, you can travel in space-time, and use pod equipment to interact with earth's physical fields. You are not tied to an anchor point such as a crystalline object.

"While we are in the laboratory we appear only to exist in four dimensions and have the bodysuit illusion. Your bodysuit and pod illusion will travel from this laboratory as your perception travels. That perceptual travel is instantaneous. You will perceive that you have traveled to Earth and be able to explore at will. However, your Earth travel will be limited by the physics of Earth. For instance, your pod can't travel faster than the speed of light.

"Is it possible for me to get stuck in the physical world?" I asked.

No," replied Dr. Ev. "We've learned how to take care of that. Your bodysuit may get stuck, but you will reappear here, outside this building."

"That's good," I replied. "What happens to the bodysuit?"

"You could control it from here for awhile if you wish, and make it walk around on Earth. Without being refueled, bodysuits do not last long. In a previous project, we had to leave a few bodysuits on Earth after an equipment malfunction. For some unknown reason, Earthlings collected them and hid them away.

"When you are in the pod, the machine will begin tumbling. It will tumble faster until you suddenly perceptually break free. You will immediately perceptually appear in your programmed destination, Earth, and be able to steer yourself around as if you existed in that physical reality.

"The pod's computer is operated by release 8.5 of the heuristically programmed algorithm. We call it HAL 8.5. The computer is a genetically engineered organism similar to your Knowledge Plate. After you are strapped in the pod, you will place your hands on the control panel of the pod. HAL will respond to steering and navigation thought commands. Your left hand controls time and your right hand controls where you are in space. When you are ready to return, think of this Laboratory, click your heels together, and HAL will bring you back.

"Since your travels will be in eight dimensions, Earthlings will not be able to observe you with their eyes or any of their radar detection devices. In some locations, there are earth-field disturbances that will make you visible. HAL can sense this and speed you out of the disturbance. Earthlings seem to be used to this and ignore the sightings."

We walked the gantry steps to the level of the pod and across the bridge to the entrance. Dr. Ev showed me where to place my hands and feet, nodded 'goodbye,' walked back across the bridge and pressed a red button. As the bridge drew back, I heard a voice.

HAL said, "Greetings Mason, and welcome aboard Earth Tour 593. Please keep your seatbelt fastened at all times because we may experience field disturbances. I will be your pilot today as we perceptually travel to Earth. After the triple rotator reaches speed, you will experience a moment of no perceptions and then we will be at your destination.

"I will give you steering lessons after we arrive. Earth space-time coordinates will be something you will automatically know. Do I have your permission to close the pod door now?"

Yes, I thought. The door closed, and the machine began to rotate. At first I was rotating and seeing Dr. Ev pass by. Then it began to speed up, to tumble. Things became a gray blur. A paralyzing vibration went through the strange bodysuit I inhabited. I had the sensation of great noise, then blackness, and then white and quiet.

HAL said, "We have arrived at our destination, Earth. The time here, as they believe time to exist, is fourteen thousand years before what Dave and Raven perceive as the present.

"Out of the left window of the pod you can see the blue and white planet. We begin Tour 593 here to give you a view of the overall planet and to start steering exercises.

Please use your intention to rotate the pod to be facing Earth. . . . Fine, now practice moving in all three directions. . . . Now, let's move down toward the planet. No, start slowly at first. . . . Now speed up and aim for that hole in the clouds. Slow down as we drop below the clouds. . . . Let's get a little lower and then stop. . . . Fine."

I saw an ocean, a valley, and then an ice-covered range of mountains.

HAL continued, "Use your intention to move closer to the mountains. There, that's fine. You're doing very well, Mason. Intend to move later in their time dimension. Start slowly."

The ice melted, and barren peaks appeared. Great ice flows slid down the mountains, carving valleys and shearing cliffs. As the ice melted, forests grew and rivers carved the landscape. Small villages appeared and filled the air with smoke from their campfires. The early inhabitants were replaced by others, driving cars.

And then the changes stopped.

HAL said, "Well done! We're now in what Earthlings perceive as the present. From here we would have to move into probable futures. This tour is not authorized to travel there. You've learned to travel in Earth time very well. Let's now move in space. Dr. Ev has found a suitable space-time segment for your experiment. We'll move there now."

I saw a green landscape of rolling hills.

HAL said, "Intend to move closer to the landscape. . . . Good! That is close enough. The space coordinate is called England and the time dimension is what they consider the present. See that area over there with the circles of standing stones and the Earthlings swarming around them? That is part of an ongoing experiment outside of our allowable space-time travel authorization.

"Intend to move us higher. . . . That is far enough. You can get a license to study the area you can see here except for those blank spots that are set aside for other's experiments. May I suggest that we move to where your study subjects reside?"

I intended to move to that place Ravi and Dave had called the Mojave. I traveled over the desert and then the pod shuddered.

HAL interrupted, "I must take control now. We have entered an earth-field disturbance where we are being observed."

The landscape blurred as we sped away.

Chapter 11

Back In L.A.

As they entered their condo in Playa Vista overlooking the Ballona wetlands, north of LAX, Ravi and Dave went into the kitchen and set down the bags of groceries. Ravi went into the living room, twirled around and said, "It's great to be home again. I love the desert, but I need a civilization break once in a while."

To the bold-colored abstract paintings on the dark blue walls she said, "Hello paintings, nice to see you again."

She opened the curtains and looked at the wetlands spreading west two miles toward the ocean and said, "Hi, birdies, I'll see you soon."

She went back into the kitchen and helped Dave put away the groceries.

After running her hand over the granite counters, she said, "I miss my kitchen after we've been in the desert a while."

Dave poured them each a glass of wine. They went into the living room and dropped onto the big cushy brown leather sofa.

"Where shall we go for dinner? Ravi asked. "We don't get to say that very often in the desert."

"I was thinking Ethiopian," Dave replied with a smile, knowing it was not high on Ravi's list of favorites.

"Let's go to the marina, have some fish, and look at some water."

"Deal."

They sat at an outdoor table at The Seafarer, on a balcony overlooking the marina and enjoyed the fresh, humid ocean breeze. They gazed at the matching blue sail covers on the rows of sailboats and sipped Mai Tais.

Their salads came, and Ravi made little sounds of delight as they ate.

"It's good to be back in L.A. At least until you have to drive somewhere," Ravi observed.

"Raven!" They looked up to see a tall, supercilious lady with long blond-streaked hair, who obviously spent a lot of time in a salon. She was wearing a designer dress, expensive heels, and carrying a Gucci purse. "How good to see you again! You let your hair grow. Charming! And, this must be Mr. Willard. How do you do! I'm Clarice Dorn."

Dave rose, took her hand, and said, "Dave Willard."

Ravi smiled and said. "How is that lovely daughter of yours doing? She must be a sophomore now. She went to Barnard College in New York, didn't she?"

"Yes, she still talks about you. She said that one of her English professors was almost as good as you. Beverly Hills High School misses you. Just the other day, Edith Eaton was lamenting the fact that you were not still there for her son. She said you were on sabbatical, writing the great American novel."

"That's right. I live in the desert north of L.A. not far from the house Aldous Huxley lived in. The desert is a great place to create."

"Oh, you must tell me about that sometime," said Clarice as she glanced over her shoulder to a distinguished looking man in a business suit being seated at a table. "You must call me as soon as the book comes out. I'll arrange a book signing for you at the club. Lots of important people can be there. Good publicity, and maybe a movie deal!"

She took Ravi's hand. "Please keep in touch! A pleasure to meet you, Mr. Willard." She turned and rushed off.

Ravi slouched a little and said, "My worst fear! The mothers and other teachers at Beverly High hold me in such great esteem. What if my novel isn't good enough?

"Some of my college friends have written novels that have sold well. I can't even think up a good short story. I've been trying for months. Nothing! I'm stuck in the present participle of 'writing a novel.' Still, no words on paper.

"Now, we're off to England. I need to set a deadline to either come up with a story or go back to teaching high school. Maybe I need to admit I'm not a writer. Maybe I should write a scholarly book of literary criticism, expand my master's thesis."

Dave took her hand. "I love you. We don't need their judgments. Write a book you love, doing it from the heart. You're the only critic that matters. What you're doing now is important to us, to me, being together."

Ravi wiped a small tear from her eye as their main courses came.

Soon, Ravi was smiling again, saying, "Oh, this is good. Breathing the ocean breeze as you eat seafood adds to the taste."

They were looking at the dessert menu when a tall man with black hair and graying temples walked up and said, "Dave Willard! Great to see you!" He eyed Ravi.

Dave stood up. "Jeremy Stephens, what a surprise! Jeremy, this is my wife, Ravi. Ravi, Jeremy was opposing counsel on a patent case I tried in Detroit."

While still ogling Ravi, Jeremy said, "I heard you left Bracken and Stevens."

Dave took out a business card and handed it to Jeremy. "I'm doing something a little different now."

Jeremy studied the card and then said, "A Silicon Valley, Palo Alto address. How do you like it up there? That place is a patent attorney's dream."

Dave replied, "I'm running a foundation sponsoring research, mostly mathematical research. No litigation or patent work yet. My home office is up there, but I spend most of my time down here."

"Well, that is Bracken and Stevens' loss, and also my loss of a worthy opponent. I have to run now. I'm meeting a client. I see him being seated over there. Keep in touch!"

As Jeremy walked away, Ravi looked at Dave who was scrunched down in his chair thinking *What if he finds out what I'm doing, investigating crop circles?*

"There you go again," Ravi scolded. "You're all moat and castle. Let down that drawbridge and let me in!"

"I'm sorry. Seeing Jeremy makes me worry about where this is all headed. He'd be delighted to know that I've been talking to aliens and chasing after kooks in crop circles. He would jump at the chance to damage my reputation as a science-oriented attorney. The time may come when I might need to go back to being a litigator."

Ravi said, "Well, you're alien to me right now. Come back!"

"Okay!" Dave replied. "You caught me again. I really shouldn't worry. Working for the Colson Foundation is fun, and I get to deal with some brilliant and fascinating people."

"I remember you recently saying that it is nice to deal with people who are all on your side," said Ravi. "No opponents trying to trip you up."

"When my Colson foundation work is over I might find other foundations that press the limits of science. Still, I worry about losing my credibility with my old peer group."

Ravi studied the desert menu for a moment and then said, "Here, at the Marina, I have to observe that we both seem to be in the same boat."

Dave laughed. With a smile, Ravi said, "I'm sorry, I couldn't resist. I think some crème brûlée will fix all this.

Chapter 12

Back From The Tour

As we sped away from the Mojave where HAL had taken control, HAL said, "This concludes our Perceptual Earth Tour. We will be returning to the laboratory now. It has been a pleasure to have you aboard Tour 593 today. We hope you had a pleasant trip and will travel with us again. Please check your seatbelt as we will experience some turbulence as we change dimensions. The pod door will open as soon as it is safe to disembark."

Things became a gray blur. A paralyzing vibration went through my bodysuit. I had the sensation of great noise, then blackness, and then white and quiet. I heard the rotating machine slow down and felt it stop. I saw Dr. Ev press the green button on the gantry control panel and a drawbridge extended to the pod.

The pod door opened, and HAL said, "Please watch your step. Enjoy your visit here or at your final destination."

Dr. Ev beamed and said, "How was the tour?"

"That was amazing!" I replied. "HAL was a great guide. My favorite spot was viewing what HAL called the Colosseum. We scanned through the times of it's construction and then used as a place for fifty-thousand Earthlings to watch brutal tribal amusements of people being killed. It then was a quarry for rock thieves, and eventually became a place of curiosity for travelers.

"We also visited pyramids, but only during the latest two eons Earthlings call millennia. HAL said we were not allowed to go much farther back in what they call time because of Galaxy 356 governing body restrictions. HAL said many of what the Earthlings call very old sites are part of an ongoing experiment and are not available for students to visit."

Dr. Ev said, "I can only tell you that the Galaxy 356 governing body has licensed regions on Earth for exclusive experimental use by many planetary civilizations. The pyramids are part of such an experiment. The licenses are for geographic spaces, such as around the pyramids, for particular spans of time, in this case, the fifty millennia before when you visited.

"Our middle school student projects are limited to a half millennia over spaces not taken by other experimenters. What else did you observe on your tour?"

"Around two and a half millennia, in what they consider the past, they built huge temples, magnificent buildings made from white rock material," I said. "I don't quite understand why they built these."

You are an observant student, Mason," said Dr. Ev. Of the three hundred civilizations we've observed, Earth is the only place where tribes create mythologies with deities. Earthlings assign great power to these gods, supposing the gods can interact and control the tribe's daily lives and welfare. Earthlings erected the marble temples to their patron gods. They hoped to gain favor and support in their wars with other tribes. The tribes also believed there were wars between the gods, gods conquering other gods. Earthlings erected temples to be on the right side."

I asked, "Why do Earthlings create that reality?"

"We've no idea," Dr. Ev replied, "Some believe it is programmed into their DNA.

"In your Earthlings 1a course, you are expected to get a general understanding of this behavior. Your Middle School Science Experiment should be designed to show tribal behavior. You may wish to use a device that I've been developing."

"What does this device do?" I asked.

Dr. Ev replied, "When unassisted by any device, we can only travel to Earth perceptually. We can't do anything that uses energy such as moving things around. We communicate only information when we 'talk' with Earthlings."

I said, "I understand. I interact only with the electrical activity in their brains and produce the illusions of seeing a spark of light and hearing words. I've learned how to do it with two of them at once."

"That's a very good ability," said Dr. Ev. "We've now made a device that takes it a step farther. We can interact with the earth's electromagnetic fields. We create templates in the electrical charges in their clouds. The charged clouds interact with Earth's local electromagnetic energies and produce microwaves. Our templates direct the microwaves to burn patterns in vegetation."

"If I understand this right," I began, "we can't send energy from here to Earth, it's too far, but we can send information that organizes earth energies to do things."

"That's the right idea," Dr. Ev said. Here at the Institute, we've mathematicians who worked it all out with eight-dimensional mathematics. Much later in your studies you may wish to work in that lab. You don't need to master all of that for your experiment.

"I've traveled in HAL 8.5 and tested places and times where the weather and soil composition are right to burn simple circles. I understand HAL took you to the space-time coordinate in what the

Earthlings call England. I mapped that area and found conditions are acceptable for experiments. HAL 8.5 can only burn simple circles. HAL release 8.6, which is in testing right now will be able to make more complex patterns.

I felt a little frightened as I commented, "Can I learn enough to do this ?"

"HAL will guide you through the operational procedures when you begin making circles. First, I would like you to prepare your detailed Middle School Science Experiment Plan. After it's approved by your proctor, Mr. Ob, we can get a student experimental license from the Galaxy 356 governing body. Be sure to pick space-times that can show a variety of Earthling tribal behaviors."

"Thank you," I said. "I'm excited to get started."

"As you leave, go back to the locker room and leave your body-suit. Anytime you return, use the same bodysuit."

As I walked my bodysuit back to the locker room, I thought, *I now understand why the study of Earthlings is a required course. Their culture and customs are so unique.*

CHAPTER 13

Security Clearance

Dave checked his phone before they left The Seafarer. and said, "I have a message from Colson that a Mr. Burton wants to meet with us tomorrow at ten o'clock. He said both of us."

"Who is he?" asked Ravi.

"He's Colson's security consultant. Colson, being a venture capitalist in Silicon Valley, is a target for all kinds of industrial espionage. Burton is the spooky guy that does all of Colson's counter-espionage, scans offices and airplanes for bugs, checks out people, and things like that. I understand he had worked for one of the government intelligence agencies before he formed his own company. You're in for a real treat. I'll reply okay."

Within a few seconds, Colson sent a reply.

"Colson said Burton will send me a message telling us where to meet tomorrow morning."

"Does he have any drones?" asked Ravi.

"If he does we'll never find out. It's probably about our trip to England. He's paid to be paranoid for Colson."

❋ ❋ ❋ ❋ ❋ ❋

The next morning Ravi conducted research on her laptop,while Dave worked on a research grant. The phone rang, he answered, and said, "Yes, that's nearby. In a 'few minutes' is fine. Okay, I'll bring our passports. We're on our way."

Ravi inquired, "Burton? Why does he want our passports? Are we in danger of being prevented from leaving the country?"

"I'll have to ask him about that. He wants to meet us at the entrance to the freshwater marsh of the wetlands down Jefferson Boulevard from here. Do you remember that bench overlooking the marsh where we had a picnic and watched birds last fall?"

"Yes, that was fun. Is he a birder?"

"No, I don't think so. He just likes to meet in isolated public places that can't be bugged or observed. It's the paranoid thing at work."

They drove to the trail entrance, walked a short distance to a bench overlooking a pond, and sat down. Ravi took out her birding binoculars. Dave looked at his watch.

"This pond would be a good place to dump bodies," commented Ravi. "Are you sure about Burton?"

"He's okay," replied Dave.

Ravi looked relieved and then, peering through her binoculars, said, "I see a snowy egret, and over there is a blue heron."

"Mr. Willard?" Dave rose and turned to greet Mr. Burton, an intimidating presence. He was tall, with jet black hair, and a rugged sun-wrinkled stern lantern-jawed face, wearing a dark blue business suit, mirrored aviator sunglasses, and carrying a briefcase.

"Raven, this is Mr. Burton."

Burton nodded his head in acknowledgment and then motioned for them to sit down. He sat next to Dave and then said, "Mr. Colson has been opening up some of his contacts in England.

You may visit some acquaintances of his in the military or go to some of their facilities. You may need clearances that require filling out a form that lists your parents, siblings, former places of residence, and organizations you have belonged to.

Dave thought, *This is not what I need now. Wasting time trying to figure out all the places I have ever lived.*

Burton continued, "Normally, you would fill out the forms and then someone in the government would check them against data bases and talk to present and former associates. That can be time-consuming. I filled out the forms for you using the same data bases the government would check against and other easily available information. I interviewed former associates before you were hired."

He took two iPads out of his briefcase and said, "The forms are prepared as word processing documents in these tablets. Each of yours is ready for your review. He opened an application on each tablet as he handed them to Dave and Ravi.

"Review these filled-out forms and tell me if any corrections need to be made. Add any organizations that are not listed."

Dave asked, "Do you want us to correct the form as we read it?"

"You may do that if you wish. Tell me as you do. Please hand me your passports."

Dave handed him the passports and asked, "Why do you need these?"

Burton replied, "I want to make sure they haven't expired and are up to date."

Dave began reading the iPad forms and thought, *This is spooky. They have all the addresses I've ever had—including when I was at the university—my parent's and siblings names, the hospital I was born in and, heck, I don't remember this—my Boy Scout Troop*

Number! They missed some of the clubs I belonged to in college, but come to think of it, most of them were informal, not on university records.

Ravi grew very anxious as she read. *How can they know all of this? I don't remember all these addresses of where I lived in college. This is frightening. What does this have to do with crop circles? Who is this Burton Guy?*

Burton looked through the passports as Dave and Ravi reviewed the forms. In about half an hour, they were finished reading and making a few corrections on the tablets. Mr. Burton had them sign the forms with a stylus.

He then said, "Dave, Your passport is about to expire. Raven, yours needs to be updated to your married name." He dug into his briefcase, produced two passport applications, and handed them to Dave and Ravi. "Sign on the bottom. We'll fill in the rest and renew them for you."

He took a small camera from his suit pocket and said, "You'll both need new passport pictures." He quickly and expertly photographed each of them in turn. "Have you decided when you would like to leave for England?"

"We were thinking about leaving in mid-June and staying for five days," Dave replied. "We don't have any detailed plans."

"Colson has asked me to make travel arrangements," Burton offered. "We'll provide a tour guide and lodging through contacts we have in England. Will that be acceptable to you?"

Dave looked at Ravi, who nodded, and said, "Yes, but I already booked airline reservations."

"I'll take care of them to make sure they fit with the tour guide's schedule. I'll return your passports with a detailed itinerary and tickets after I make arrangements.

"I'll also send you copies of the forms you just filled out. There's nothing more you need to do in this matter. Everything will be taken care of." He stood up, shook Dave's hand, nodded to Ravi and said, "Thank you for your attention to these formalities."

He disappeared down the path.

Ravi grabbed onto Dave's arm and said, "Do you feel that something has just been taken from us besides our passports? Our identity is now on one piece of paper. Dave, is there something about you that you haven't told me about?"

Dave looked at her and smiled, "I'll let you read my form after Burton sends it. I'll be happy to answer any questions. They didn't take our identity away. That's the way things are now. It's all out there in data bases.

"I am only a lowly teacher. Why do they have files on me?"

"Everyone is in the files. People would be very suspicious if you were not in the data bases.

"Colson has Burton check out people in the companies that come to him for investments. The information on Burton's form looks like they want to make sure we are who we are and that our identities weren't made up five years ago."

Ravi became wide-eyed and said, "Do they think we're spies?"

"Probably not. In Burton's world, they're routinely cautious. Remember, he's a paid paranoid."

Ravi thought for a minute and then said, "I need to calm down. I think I'll walk around and do some birding. You can go on home. I'll be back by lunch time."

Dave looked carefully at Ravi, then smiled and said, "Burton doesn't bother me that much. I'm sure you could use some birding right now. I'll see you at lunch."

CHAPTER 14

Gathering of Spooks

The blue staff car stopped at the mall entrance to the Pentagon. Brigadier General Anderson stepped out, walked up the steps to the reinforced glass doors, went in and put on his identification badge. After checking through the airport-like security, he walked to the right, down a mahogany-paneled hall hung with original oil paintings of historical war scenes, where he opened the door to the entrance of the stairwell.

Two flights below, he entered a hallway guarded by a Marine dressed in perfectly pressed battle fatigues, standing at attention, wearing a sidearm in a highly polished holster. The Marine saluted and said, "Good morning, sir." Please present your ID." The Marine held up the ID badge as he spent half a minute comparing the badge photo with the general's face. He examined it under a UV light and then said, "Have a nice day," while pressing a buzzer that unlocked the door.

General Anderson walked through a hall of bare walls covered with a gray felt-looking material that he knew absorbed sound and radio waves. Turning through an unmarked gray door into another small anteroom, he met another Marine in uniform. After another ID inspection, General Anderson went to the wall, typed a pin number into a keypad and stared into a retinal scanner. The lock buzzed, he opened the metal door, and entered the conference room.

Major General Hopkins greeted him and said, "Max, how good to see you again. Any mutinies among all those drones under your command? How are Elaine, and your son Bill?"

General Anderson returned the joke, "I'm happy to report discipline and morale are high. Elaine is great. She's off visiting our grandchildren in Florida where Bill works for Disney World."

"Max, I'd like you to meet a new man on our Dragonfly Team. This is Avery Thomas from the agency. I believe you know Jack from the FBI. All four of us are Dragonfly cleared. He shook Avery's hand then turned to Jack from the FBI and said, "Jack, I'll let you be the lead on this meeting. Hoppy, you can make the required statement."

The four men sat down around the small metal conference table and then General Anderson stated, "This is a Dragonfly meeting and everything discussed here is Dragonfly unless otherwise identified. Jack, you may proceed."

Jack unwrapped a double-sealed envelope and took out his notes. He began, "As everyone is aware, the Air Force Project Bluebook was shut down in 1969 for security reasons. Since 1969, Dragonfly has since been the archive for data on UFO sightings and artifacts collected from possible UFO crash sites. It is also the home of an interagency team conducting a study of the possible threat and international political implications of alien contacts. Dragonfly is embedded in a top-secret drone program hangar in Palmdale. It's a high priority espionage target for both foreign and domestic technical and political interests.

We have an agent who has infiltrated a domestic organization funded by U.S. political interests intent on revealing what is known about extraterrestrial contacts and surveillance of our planet. The agent is to report any imminent attempt to breach the security at our Dragonfly facility. If an infiltration is planned, she is to call a secret telephone number and leave a coded message.

"One week ago a female called at 18:23 hours and left a message that when decoded informed us of a planned physical infiltration of our Dragonfly hangar. A full security deployment was undertaken, but no intruders were observed that night or during the next week.

"She was identified by her caller ID as Raven Willard. A data search showed she is married to Dave Willard. Earlier that day, a routine test flight of one of our surveillance drones observed a car registered to them driving to an abandoned airline terminal on the Air Force Plant 42 airport near Palmdale. They met a Learjet that Air Traffic Control identified.

"We checked our agency sources and Mr. and Mrs. Willard have never applied for a security clearance. She appears to be a high school English teacher. She didn't show up in any of our records. Her husband is the director of a nonprofit foundation. We haven't determined what the foundation does. It could be suspicious.

"From FAA flight records, we identified the airplane as owned by the Colson Capital Corporation, an international venture capital firm. From FAA records, we also identified the pilot, and co-pilot, a former Alaskan bush pilot, and a former U.S. Navy pilot, neither of whom ring any bells. Vince Colson appeared in our records and has a current Top Secret security clearance. He may have tickets to special programs, but he is not Dragonfly.

"We've connected these data points: We've someone who lives near a top secret drone facility sending coded messages to a secure telephone. That person has an association with a nonprofit corporation that could be a cover for clandestine activities. That person and her husband are associated with an international businessman with high-level contacts in many countries."

"Together these data points looks suspicious. We thought we should get CIA involved. Avery, what did you come up with?"

Avery took off his glasses, cleaned them with a white handkerchief, put them back on, and started, "She isn't one of ours either. No record of her or her husband in our files. Colson is another story. Let's say he has many friends at The Agency who talk to him after some of his trips abroad. He has some special tickets at The Agency. He's highly connected.

"Colson might be an intelligence target and the people in this foundation part of the scheme. As a precaution, I think we should conduct a background investigation on them. I'll talk to Colson's friends at The Agency and make it happen."

General Anderson replied, "Too much smoke for me. We had better see if there's a fire here that we need to take care of. Avery, can you take care of this? Do whatever you need to get Homeland Security interested without letting them know any of us are involved."

General Anderson turned to General Hopkins and said, "Hoppy, I'll be lead on this and keep you informed. Jack and Avery will keep me up to speed."

Both Jack and Avery nodded in agreement. General Hopkins looked at them and then said, "Okay, thanks everyone for your diligence. All precautions should be taken when Dragonfly is involved."

As they left the conference room, Max slapped General Anderson on the back and said, "Good to see you again. Let's get together for a round of golf next time you're in town. My best to Elaine."

CHAPTER 15

Ravi And Mason

After Dave had left, Ravi walked about a quarter of a mile on the path next to the marsh. Spotting a bird she didn't recognize, she sat down on a nearby bench. As she was studying the bird through her binoculars, she heard, "Good morning, as you know time to exist. It is a beautiful morning in this place you have chosen to visit."

Ravi looked around as her heart raced. Was Burton back? Then, she saw a bright blue spark of light in a discarded clear glass bottle. She felt relieved and said, "Mason?"

"Yes, that is the name by which you know me. I come in peace and love, don't be frightened."

Ravi relaxed and joked, "You scared me! I didn't recognize you in your new outfit."

Ravi got up from of the bench and sat down cross-legged near the bottle. She read the label on the bottle, "Rocket Body Fuel Energy Drink." "Why did you choose this bottle? Is there a special message for me on the label?"

Mason replied, "I chose this bottle because it is near you and has a crystalline form. It is easier for me to focus my presence in crystalline objects."

"Why are you here?" Ravi asked. "Are you a birder?"

"No. Although there are many beautiful creatures on your planet, studying them is not my reason for contacting you at this time, as you believe time to exist."

"Then, why are you here?" she asked.

"I come in friendship, to communicate with you and get to understand your species more."

Ravi said, "By saying species, are you referring to mankind?"

Mason replied, "I'm not sure about the meaning in your language about man-kind. I'm interested in the expression of male and female energies as it occurs in both types of physical forms. I've observed your species in action over millennia, and I would not describe it as generally kind. I recall the Roman amusements in their Colosseum and the many wars between tribes. Your species is not always kind."

Ravi thought for a second. "I should have said humans. How do you know about the Romans?"

Mason paused and then said, "I've traveled in both space and time over your planet and observed many amazing things as a part of learning about Earth and Earthlings."

"Can you travel through space and time at will?" asked Ravi.

"Yes. I can perceptually travel at will to visit you here, and as you say, now. I can also visit you at coordinates you would describe as the past."

Ravi looked startled as she said, "Can you tell me about my future?"

Mason answered, "I'm here on what you might call a student visa. We are not allowed to discuss your future." He paused and then continued, "I sense that you are uncertain about the ideas of space-time. I would like to tell you more about them if you are interested."

"Oh, that's okay," Ravi replied quickly. "I'm happy to let my husband worry about all that science stuff. It won't confuse me because I can ignore it. I can accept that you're here and speak to me."

"That is an admirable attitude," said Mason. "I sense that you are embarked on an investigation where a little more knowledge of space-time might be of value to you. Also, I would like to get your opinion on a simple analogy I've been developing. Would you like to hear it?"

Ravi grimaced a little and then said, "Sure, I'm game."

First," Mason began, "We have your three common dimensions. Your iPad can tell you your current location in terms of the three dimensions of latitude, longitude, and altitude. Now for time: your iPad can tell you the current time. That time, as you perceive it, is only a now point on your history timeline that stretches from the past into the future. In space dimensions, you might measure the separation of two things in terms of, as you say, feet, miles or degrees longitude. In the dimension of time, you measure the separation of things that happened a week ago and things that are happening now in minutes, hours, or days.

"Having a space dimensions is a convenient way to keep everything from happening in the same place. Having a time dimension is a handy way to keep everything from happening at once. Space-time is handy for keeping everything sorted out."

Ravi said, "I understand that. Although, I haven't ever thought of a separation in time as a dimension." She paused and then continued. "Yesterday I was sitting in my living room reading. My iPad would have given me a different location and time, different space-time coordinates. I guess I understand that. But you say time is an illusion. How does that fit in?"

Mason explained, "In your reality, you can travel to a memory in space and time and create the perception of being there. Your scientists have not found any place in your physical brain that can store all the videos of memories you have accumulated. Somehow, you can perceptually recall and re-experience those memories. Can you recall a memory which you consider special?"

Ravi thought a second then said, "I remember my sixth birthday when my father brought home a puppy. We named him Corky. I can remember how soft and squirmy he felt and even how he smelled."

"While you are in the recall of that illusion," Mason commented, "now, was then, when you had the experience. As you go through your daily life, you may recall many memories. Each memory has its own now, and its space-time coordinates."

Ravi wrinkled her forehead and looked puzzled as she said, "I guess I understand that. I need to think about it some more. Do you mean that we don't store all of our memories in our head? Do you mean that when we remember, we perceptually space-time travel to when and where they happened?"

"I will now leave you to ponder that question," Mason replied. "If you desire, we can discuss this further at, as you say, another time."

Ravi replied, "You mean, at another set of space-time coordinates?"

"You got it!" exclaimed Mason as the blue spark of light in the Rocket Body Fuel Energy Drink bottle went out.

Descanso

The next day, at breakfast, Dave said, "I have to meet with Candice Montgomery to talk about her Colson grant. I agreed to meet her this afternoon at her home in Altadena. Would you like to come along? It might be boring math stuff."

"I'd love to see her again. We spent a lot of time together at the Foundation's meeting in Aspen last fall." Can we stop at Descanso Gardens on the way to Altadena?" asked Ravi.

"That's a great idea!" Dave replied. "I haven't been there for years. I'd love for us to see it together. All the azaleas and camellias will be blooming."

Ravi spoke with excitement as she said, "Let's leave here early and stop for a couple of hours on our way. I need a 'nature in full bloom fix.' I'll make us some sandwiches and we can turn this into a picnic."

They threaded the freeways from their home to Altadena, past the urban sprawl of Central L.A., past the forest of high-rise office buildings of downtown, out the tree-lined Arroyo Seco Parkway. At the edge of the mountains, they came to the Descanso Gardens exit.

Inside the gardens, Ravi said, "Here, let's go this way."

They walked a short distance and then turned onto another path that took them over an arched bridge, above koi basking in a creek, to a Japanese tea house, surrounded by cherry and plum trees in full bloom.

As they sat down on a bench underneath a tree's radiant canopy, Ravi took Dave's hand. "I love this Zen garden. It's so peaceful." After a minute, she took her hand back and looked into his eyes. She looked serene as she said, "I think I'll meditate for a while. Do you mind?"

Dave replied, "Of course, I don't mind. I'll visit the koi."

He walked to the quiet creek running by the tea house and admired the granite stonework lining the creek. The blooms of overhanging trees washed the sky with color. As he sat down on a bench he thought, *What a peaceful place.* He watched a gold and a black koi resting near the bottom, patiently waiting for something good to eat to wash by.

Dave felt Ravi's love and a glow around his heart. He thought, *This can't be real. I don't understand the physics of this energy transfer.*

Dave closed his eyes and drifted into a sort of dream state. Then he sensed someone next to him and opened his eyes. Ravi was sitting on the bench next to him, smiling, staring through him to some other place. She refocussed her gaze on him. "Oh, I hope I didn't disturb you. I've never seen you meditate like that before."

Dave rubbed his eyes and said, "I drifted off." He took her hand and said, "This is a special place. I just sat, started to feel the peaceful energy and drifted away." He thought, *Peaceful energy, metaphysics, what is happening to me? Shape up!*

Ravi said, "Don't go away on me again. Let down the drawbridge!"

In the creek, a koi quickly darted away from a shiny rock that glowed with an intense blue spark of light.

They sat, relishing their love.

After a long pause, Ravi said, "I need to get grounded. Let's walk around through the camellias."

They walked down a dirt path, under a towering canopy of oak trees providing cover for a thousand tall, radiantly blooming camellia bushes, to a clearing with a bench on the edge of a small pond.

Ravi pointed toward the bench. "Let's stop here for lunch."

Dave looked at his watch and said, "We've lots of time," and opened the sack of sandwiches he'd been carrying.

As they were eating, Ravi said, "Candice and I got to spend a lot of time talking in Aspen last fall. I loved talking to her. I compared notes with her about our Native American heritages and what it means to us. I'm anxious to see what kind of home she has. Maybe something in a stucco-southwestern style with hand woven rugs and baskets on the wall?

"She has an interesting mix of ideas, some from her academic father, who was a chemistry professor, and some from visiting her medicine-man Muscogee grandfather in Oklahoma.

Dave thought, *Here she goes again with that metaphysical garbage.*

Ravi tactfully changed the subject and said, "I'm glad to see Descanso again. It's in my novel."

Dave sat up straight, looked at Ravi, and said, "That's a surprise. I didn't know you had started writing. What's the novel about?"

"Two nights ago, kind of in a dream, the story came to me in a flash. Without waking you, I got up and wrote the whole outline down. More details have been coming to me in flashes. These gardens will be a part of it."

"Give me a hint," said Dave, "Am I in it? Are you writing about us?"

Ravi looked very stern and said, "It is no use to ask. I'm not going to tell you anything about it until it's finished. I want it to be all mine, and if we talk about it, our thoughts might get intertwined. Besides, I don't want to be subject to your scientific evaluations."

"Okay, I get it. You can't blame me for asking."

They didn't notice the blue flash from a rock in the pond.

❄ ❄ ❄ ❄ ❄ ❄

It only took a few minutes to drive from Descanso Gardens to Candice's house. Altadena is a town built on the rolling hills above Pasadena, on the border of where the land gives way to steep brush-covered mountains.

It was a beautiful day. A late spring cold front had passed through during the night, clearing out the L.A. haze and smog, making the sky sparkling blue and dotting the mountains with a procession of small, puffy clouds.

As they drove, Ravi admired and commented on the variety and architecture of homes. Victorian homes from the early days of Altadena sat next to old bungalows from the Depression era made from the prefab kits bought from Sears and Roebuck catalogs. Small tracts of late thirties houses in stucco, Mediterranean or Spanish style, added to the ambiance of the neighborhood.

When they arrived at Candice's, Ravi said, "This isn't what I was expecting. Isn't that darling, a Craftsman style? I can see it's a home that somebody loves."

Candice met them at the door. She was of average height and a rather frail build, dressed in a long, black pleated dress matching her long, straight black hair. Her bronze complexion betrayed her mixed racial heritage. Her wide, brown eyes seemed to portray a mix of great curiosity and admiration.

"Come in," she said. Welcome to 'Almost the Mountains.' Ravi, it's good to see you again. I guess the last time I saw you was in Aspen."

"I love your house!" replied Ravi. "Oh, this is just perfect. I love the Craftsman-era homes. You've done a wonderful job of restoration and decoration."

Candice beamed at the compliment and said, "Would you like a tour?"

"Yes!" answered Ravi.

Candice picked up a folder from the table, handed it to Dave, and said, "You can start looking at my report while Ravi and I tour the house."

A flash of blue light sparkled in a crystal hanging in the window.

A few minutes later they returned and Candice said, "Ravi, Dave and I need to talk theory for a while. Would you like to explore the back yard or sit on the patio for a while?"

Ravi replied, "You don't have to entertain me. I can read my book in that big inviting recliner on the patio."

Candice nodded and said, "Go outside and relax. I'll bring you a big iced tea."

Ravi read for a while, took a nap, and woke when she heard the screen door slam.

Candice and Dave came out the door.

"That was great!" said Dave to Candice. "I can't wait to report the part about plasmas to Colson. It ties right in with what we've read about ball lightning and crop circles."

"What was that all about?" asked Ravi.

Candice sat down at the table and said, "I was telling Dave about how eight-dimensional math predicts plasmas that can form ball lightning. Before this, many people have observed it, but nobody had any explanation for it."

"Is that important?" asked Ravi.

"Only to those of us who make a living thinking about such things," Candice said with a mysterious smile.

The bright blue spark of light in the crystal hanging in the window flashed and went out.

CHAPTER 13

Dragonfly

The lock buzzed on the metal door of a super-secret conference room in a lower basement of the Pentagon. General Anderson entered.

General Hopkins greeted him saying, "Max, let's get started. I believe you've had a Dragonfly security introduction to everyone here. I'll state that this is a Dragonfly meeting and everything discussed here is Dragonfly classification unless otherwise identified. Max, you may proceed."

The two generals and two civilians, Avery from the CIA and Jack from the FBI, sat down at the metal table.

General Anderson began. "Jack will give us an update of the security situation we reported on at our last meeting."

Jack unwrapped a double-sealed envelope and took out his notes. He began, "Since 1969, Dragonfly has been the archive for data on UFO sightings and artifacts collected from UFO crash sites. It is also the home of an interagency team doing a study of the possible threat and international political implications of alien contacts. Dragonfly is a high priority espionage target for both foreign and domestic, technical and political, interests.

We believe we have uncovered a married couple who may be trying to obtain Dragonfly information. They work for a nonprofit corporation funded by an international businessman named Colson. He has access to several of our highly classified research programs. He has Dragonfly clearance but has only needed to know about a small part of the program. We've grown concerned that the female might be an agent trying to penetrate some of the programs to which Colson has access..

"We had a full routine background check made on the female and her husband. They both came up clean. She had recently been a teacher at Beverly Hills High School. I asked Avery to see what he might find. Avery, explain."

Avery took off his glasses, cleaned them with a white handkerchief, and began, "I began by checking the NSA telephone call data base to see if she called any of the numbers on our watch list. Bingo! We found she made many calls to foreign people of concern to us in Beverly Hills.

"Last June, she made two calls to an unlisted, residential number of a wealthy, prominent Iranian family. Someone in that household frequently calls an individual in Iran associated with the Iranian uranium processing activity.

"Last May, she also made a call to the unlisted number of a Beverly Hills residence of part of the Saudi Royal Family. Someone at that number often calls a known Saudi international arms dealer.

"Several times in the preceding six months, she called unlisted numbers of the residence of a wealthy Beverly Hills family on our watch list. Someone in that household calls the Israel residence of a family known to include members of the Mossad Department of Collections, which conducts Israeli espionage."

Avery paused and looked at Jack.

Jack said, "Thank you, Avery. Based on this evidence we were able to obtain a court order allowing us to monitor the female's and her husband's telephone calls and internet activity. She has stopped her calls to the mentioned people in Beverly Hills. She has apparently completed whatever business she was trying to conduct. We found that she and her husband had booked airline flights to London this summer. No arrangements have been made for hotels or further travel. We don't know who they are meeting there and what other countries they plan to visit.

"I recommend that we assign Avery's people the task of keeping track of them when they go abroad."

Avery answered, "I'll take care of that sir."

Everyone looked at General Hopkins who said, "What do you think, Max?"

General Anderson replied, "Too much smoke for me. We had better see if there is a fire to go with the smoke. Avery, can you take care of this? Make sure you get State and Homeland Security interested. Everyone comfortable with this?" He looked around and then said, "Good! This meeting is concluded."

Avery Meets With Burton

Avery hurried across the street into the round park at the center of Dupont Circle, one of the traffic roundabouts common in Washington D.C. He walked by a few homeless people, others sitting, reading, or eating sack lunches, and a man who was juggling. He sat on a vacant bench and opened his lunch.

A black-haired man, wearing reflective sunglasses and a dark business suit joined him. He opened a sack and started throwing bread crumbs to vigilant birds. "Avery," he said, "it's your nickel."

Without seeming to notice his companion, Avery replied, "Those two we did the background investigations on, who work for the Colson Foundation . . ."

"Yes?" replied Burton.

"You said they were going to England to investigate crop circles. They'll need a tour guide. Here's a name." He laid a business card on the bench. "She's from MI6 and will make all of their tour arrangements."

Burton threw another handful of crumbs to the birds and said, "Anything else?"

"Have a good day." Avery folded up his lunch sack and walked away.

Burton threw some more crumbs to the birds as he slipped the card into his pocket. A few minutes later he crossed the street from Dupont Circle to the Metro subway entrance. As Burton rode down the escalator, he read the card, "Elise Witherton, Southern England, Sacred Site Guide."

Avery walked a few blocks down Connecticut Avenue to a dirty brownstone brick building, climbed the stairs, and went through a door labeled Wilson Building. He climbed two flights of stairs and knocked on a frosted glass door labeled with 213.

"Yes?" he heard. "What do you want?"

"Gas Company," Avery replied.

The door lock buzzed, and Avery stepped into a room filled with disorderly shelves of electronic devices and a table piled with thick, loosely-bound manuals and documents. A pudgy young black-haired woman sat viewing three computer screens. She looked up at Avery with a slight leer and said, "To what do I owe the pleasure of seeing you again, Mr. Smith?"

"Another job," Avery answered as he removed a sealed envelope from his coat pocket and handed it to the woman.

She opened the envelope and took out a stack of hundred dollar bills wrapped in a few sheets of paper.

Avery said "the sheets of paper are profiles of two people of interest. Get me the files on their personal computers containing this list of key words and forward to Mr. Smith at the indicated email address. They are booked on the mentioned flight to London. Homeland Security will be interested in them."

The woman sneered as she counted the money, nodded, and said, "Too bad for them. Anything else?"

"Have a good day," said Avery as he left.

CHAPTER 19

Mason Starts His Project

After I had completed a plan for my science project, it was time to review it with Mr. Ob, my proctor. As usual, I was expected to create an earth reality illusion for the review meeting as part of my Earthlings 1a course. I decided to create a place like one I saw on the Earth Tour 593.

I created a valley carved by glaciers in a solid granite mountain. In the valley floor, I created a lush green forest, meadows blooming with wildflowers, and a meandering, sparkling river. Along the sides of the valley, I created two billowing rainbow-filled waterfalls, cascading from the high cliffs, feeding creeks flowing to join the river. In the distance, I made dark blue cloud-capped peaks. Near the entrance to the valley, I made a granite dome, sprouting little clumps of opportunistic pine trees growing in cracks.

I entered my illusion and walked up a winding trail to the peak. Mr. Ob was sitting, dressed in beaded buckskin, wearing a headband with two orange feathers stuck in the back. He sat on a boulder thumping on a small drum in his lap.

Mr. Ob turned as I approached, smiled, and said, "I'm enjoying the spectacular reality you created for our meeting. Is this based on something you saw on your last Earth tour?"

I replied, "Yes, the four-dimensional earth reality has many wonders."

Mr. Ob rubbed his hands on the buckskin and said, "My apparel is fascinating. I gather it is how the indigenous people of this place dressed. Good detail and research. You are using your Knowledge Plate well."

"I now have a plan for my science project," I announced with some pride. "I think it will be very interesting."

"I'm glad to see the enthusiasm you have," Mr. Ob said. "I'd like to hear about your plan."

"Dr. Ev has developed software-controlled devices, which can be carried in his pods, which are capable of interacting with earth fields to produce intense bursts of energy. These energy bursts can be directed to produce patterns. He has successfully made circles in a long-stemmed crop that Earthlings call wheat."

"I'm familiar with that form of vegetation," said Mr. Ob. "One of my former students made a study of what Earthlings eat."

"I plan to study how Earthlings of different tribes respond to the sudden appearance of patterns in wheat and other similar crops. I will make them at many coordinates, over what Earthlings call time.

"In the first phase of my plan, I will make a few simple circular patterns and observe the human interaction. I will test the experimental procedure to assure I can collect the data I need.

"Dr. Ev will soon have improved software for the pods that will make complicated patterns. For the second phase of my experiments, I will use that software to create many more complex patterns at many space-time locations, and study the tribal reactions."

I handed him my Knowledge Plate bookmarked to where I had inscribed my plan.

Mr. Ob read for a while, smiled, and said, "I will communicate your plan to the 356 Galaxy Governing Board's Experiment Licensing Branch. I don't think we'll have any delays in getting a middle school student experimental license as long as your plan is constrained to less than a half earth millennia and does not enter the space-times of other experiments. Dr. Ev will tell you when your plan is approved. Please visit me again after your first mission so I can get a better feel for what you are doing."

"Thank you," I said.

"I'll send you to Dr. Ev now."

I experienced a momentary flash of dull light, like being in a dense fog, and then I found myself again standing on a grass-covered slope. I put both hands on my Knowledge Plate, and the Eight-dimensional Travel Laboratory appeared. I walked through the entrance, down a short, dazzling white hall, entered the locker room, and stood in front of the bodysuit hanging neatly in my locker. I opened the door and saw a blinding flash. I was back in my gray bodysuit, again half-physical.

I walked into the main semi-physical building, past the trees, across a bridge over a small creek, and into the Vehicle Laboratory. I was getting comfortable operating a bodysuit.

In the center of the Vehicle Laboratory, in a large, dimly lit glass enclosure, a gantry enclosed a nest of girders and gimbals with a small pod in the center. This pod was slightly different from the one I had used on my Earth tour.

Dr. Ev, standing at a control console, looked up, waved at me, and gave me the slight smile that was all these bodysuits were capable of. I smiled back, although I was not sure how much showed. He said, "Congratulations! Your Middle School Science Project has been approved and licensed. Let's get started. Any questions?"

Using my bodysuit arm, I pointed to the row of pods in cradles along the wall and said, "You have quite an assortment of vehicle pods here. They weren't here when I took my Earth tour. What are they for?"

"I didn't include them in the illusion of your previous visit. They are all the same pod with different experimental add-ons. For instance, the first one is the basic pod fitted with sensors for high school students to map the earth's magnetic field."

"Do any of these carry more than one bodysuit?" I asked.

Dr. Ev's bodysuit showed a slight furrow in what you would call the forehead, and then he replied, "No, earlier in our experimental program we tried a two-bodysuit model. Having two consciousnesses in the same pod confused the control system while in the earth's field, and it crashed. The wreck caused quite a stir among the Earthlings. The 356 Galaxy Earth Park patrol had to intercede and clean up the mess. We almost lost our experimental license. Finally, we were able to negotiate the continuation of our survey, but only in single bodysuit vehicles."

Dr. Ev continued to describe each of the pods and its measurement mission. Then he pointed to the pod in the rotator gimbals at the center of the gantry. The pod had four arms with large flat plates on the end. It resembled a four-legged earth mammal. "Your pod will be controlled by the same HAL that took you on the earth tour.

"When you hover above the Earth, HAL will tell you when a suitable earth field is present. Visualize a circular pattern in the vegetation. Then make the pattern disappear with a flash of light. If the right natural earth environmental conditions occur, the circle pattern will imprint on the vegetation within a few Earth days. On our prototype test mission, we found that nighttime rainstorms were the most favorable for causing the imprints."

"Will I be able to see the results?" I asked.

"Yes," Dr. Ev replied. "HAL will transport you forward in the time dimension so you can see if a pattern forms and if any humans observe them.

"Our researchers have analyzed the data from other experiments and made a list of likely space-time places to make patterns that'll be observed by humans. HAL is programmed to visit these. HAL can take you to the selected space-times, but the rest is up to you. It will be up to you to decide whether you have produced a suitable pattern and if you have recorded a notable human reaction.

We walked over to a mock-up of the cockpit of the pod. I got in, and Dr. Ev had me go through visualization exercises ,and the simulator showed me the results. I practiced until I had a good feel for the experiment.

"I think I have it," I said. "It's not that hard."

Dr. Ev replied, "HAL can help you out if you need it."

I climbed out of the simulator as Dr. Ev said, "After you return, the data will be downloaded to your Knowledge Plate so you can go home and investigate the historical context of the data points and the human reactions. HAL can answer anything you might like to know. Any questions now?"

I thought for awhile and then answered, "I guess not, but I have a great feeling of uncertainty."

"That's normal," replied Dr. Ev. "If it weren't uncertain, it wouldn't be an experiment. HAL can bail you out of any problems.

Remember, if all else fails, click your bodysuit heels together and you will immediately be back here. Are you ready to go?"

I hesitated for a moment and then said, "Yes, let's do it!"

We walked through the glass doors to the gantry, climbed the steps, and crossed the bridge to the pod. Dr. Ev helped me get in. I placed my hands and feet on the control surfaces. I gave a thumbs up to Dr. Ev who turned and walked back across the bridge. He waved and pressed a red button. As the bridge drew back, I heard a familiar voice.

HAL said, "Greetings, Mason, and welcome aboard Earth mission 8-512, Crop Circle Creation and Observation. Please keep your seatbelt fastened at all times because we may experience field disturbances. I'll be your pilot today as we perceptually travel to Earth. After the triple rotator reaches speed, you will experience a moment of no perceptions and then we will be at your destination."

The machine began to rotate, and then sped up and tumbled. My vision became a gray blur, as a paralyzing vibration went through my bodysuit, followed by a great noise, blackness, then white, and quiet.

HAL said, "We have arrived at our destination, Earth. We are at your experimental plan location number one, the place known as southern England and the Earth date is August 2, 1880. The coordinate transformation they call altitude is one thousand feet. We are invisible to the human animals now."

I looked out the pod window and saw rolling hills covered with green vegetation punctuated by occasional houses and farm buildings. Below us, I saw widely spaced small puffy clouds, some of which had dark bands of rain dropping from them.

"I love this planet," I said. "It's so beautiful!"

Hal said, "Shall I energize the probe, Mason?"

"Yes," I said. I visualized the circle. Then, Hal moved forward in time, and I saw a rainstorm, about midnight earth time, and a circular pattern appeared in the vegetation. As HAL traveled forward in time, I saw a boy and a girl come from the nearby stone-walled, thatched-roof house and discover the crop circle. They approached the circle stealthily. My sensor recorded the girl saying, "Sure enough, we've been visited by fairies, and they must have done a dance here." The boy replied, "Oh, yes indeed. But, Pa is going to be mad as a stub-toed rooster upon seeing some of his crop is destroyed."

I recorded the girl running back to the house and bringing her mother back. Then, the father came, and they all had a lot to say. Their language was strange, so I recorded it for future analysis. I traveled forward in time and observed other visitors, their comments, and reactions.

I said, "HAL, I think we have all the data we need at this space-time coordinate. Let's move on to another point." I saw a circle of large stones standing in the distance. "Let's go there."

Hal replied, "I'm sorry, Mason, I'm afraid I can't do that."

"What's the problem?" I asked.

There was a long pause and then Hal said, "That is the site of another ongoing experiment. Our license doesn't allow us there. Shall we proceed to the preprogrammed space-time coordinate number two?"

"Fine," I replied reluctantly. I looked at the ancient circle of stones and wondered what kind of experiment that might be.

CHAPTER 20

Arrangements

Ravi and Dave walked into the kitchen of their Playa Vista condominium and started to put away the groceries they had picked up on the way home from visiting Candice. The doorbell rang. Dave answered. He came back into the kitchen, opening a FedEx envelope and said, "Here are our tickets and travel arrangements. Burton got us new passports! That saved us a lot of time."

Ravi grabbed her passport, looked inside and said, "It has the new picture Burton took. Do you think I'm gaining weight? When do we leave?"

Dave looked at the itinerary and said, "June 16, at 5:50 p.m. on American Airlines. Great! He's upgraded us to first class! He's arranged for a tour guide who'll pick us up at Heathrow. We're staying at a bed and breakfast in some place called, Pewsey, Wiltshire.

Ravi said, "Wiltshire is the county in southern England where most of the crop circles appear. This is exciting! I need to go shopping for some travel clothes."

"From the pictures I've seen in our research," Dave continued, "I don't think people dress up much to visit crop circles.

You do need a new bag. The Associate Director of the Foundation shouldn't be traveling with your old Samsonite teacher's suitcase. We might need some rain gear."

Ravi touched her hair and said, "I'd better get my hair done into a cut that works in the rain. I'll borrow some dowsing rods from my friend, Beverly. They'll come in handy. I think we need to fully experience what it's like to be inside crop circles."

Dave thought, *Right! I bet it's about as exciting as sitting in a wheat field.*

One of Ravi's quartz crystals on the mantle glowed with a blue light.

CHAPTER 21

Intelligence Work

Major General Hopkins welcomed Avery Thomas from The Agency into his private office in the Pentagon. "Good to see you again," said the General.

Avery took a seat and said, "I want to give you an update on the matter we discussed at our last project review downstairs. One of our people, who is a friend of Colson, talked to him. He's sending the couple to England to investigate ball lightning found in the vicinity of crop circles. He's cooperated with us on surveillance arrangements. I'm making arrangements for our MI6 contacts in London to provide a tour guide for Colson's people while they're in England. They'll steer the visitors away from locals who might accidentally divulge credible information about the subjects you and I have been trying to keep quiet.

General Hopkins added, "MI6 has been doing a commendable job of keeping a lid on the situation."

Avery replied, "To date, we've found no reason to be concerned that the couple has any knowledge of, or interest in, our favorite project. Colson agrees."

The General smiled and then said, "Thanks for the update, and thanks for doing it such a way that we didn't have to meet downstairs. Keep me informed."

CHAPTER 22

Mason Reports

My next meeting with Mr. Ob took place on a corner in a busy city illusion I created. Mr. Ob was standing on a corner as cars and taxi cabs roared by. Horns honked. A distant siren screamed. A crowd of people in summer business clothes flowed along the sidewalk, somehow managing to navigate as they talked and sent messages on their cell phones. Mr. Ob wore blue jeans and a black T-shirt with The Grateful Dead logo on it.

As I approached, he frowned and said, "Nice creation. I've never experienced this before. What's a Grateful Dead?"

Mason was proud to have the answer, "It's one of the contemporary religious sects of the older population who gather for ecstatic rituals. It's too busy here to communicate. I've created something called a park down this concrete path."

They were suddenly in an urban park with trees, fountains, lawns, and benches.

Mr. Ob was looking around in astonishment as he said, "This is all new to me. I've never experienced a city before. What are those animals sleeping next to those wire-framed vehicles?"

"The vehicles are filled with personal belongings and called shopping carts," I replied. "The animals are called homeless. I haven't figured out what they are for."

We sat down on a bench and I said, "I completed my first data-gathering mission. It went well." I handed him my Knowledge Plate. "Here are illusions that summarize my start at data gathering."

Mr. Ob observed the English countryside, crop circles suddenly appearing, Earthlings rushing into them and engaging in a variety of rituals. He then saw images of people arguing about crop circles and others reading books about them. He saw people coming from many lands to visit the circles.

"Good job, Mason! This is a very interesting study of earthling behavior. Please meet with me again when you have completed your data gathering."

I created the illusion of a white bird flying away.

CHAPTER 23

MI6 Meeting

Avery rode the escalator down into the Piccadilly Underground Station, walked through a bustling ticket area and then into a bookstore. He approached the clerk and asked, "Do you have a copy of Charles Dickens' *Bleak House?*

The clerk replied, "You'll find it at the end of aisle four." As Avery walked toward the isle, the clerk pressed a button under the desk that unlocked the door labeled storeroom at the end of aisle four. Avery walked through the door and was greeted by his MI6 contact, Daniel Hughes. He introduced Avery, his CIA contact, to Elise Witherton and Charles Donovan and said, "These are the people who will be guiding Colson's visitors from America in crop circle country. Ms. Witherton retired from our organization several years ago and lives in the crop circle country and keeps us informed about events there. She'll be working with Mr. Donovan our former attaché to the military organization doing black ops training in the area."

Daniel said, "Avery, why don't you outline your interests in the visitors."

Avery took off his glasses and cleaned them with a white handkerchief. "We would like these visitors from the United States,

Mr. and Mrs. Willard, to return home without gaining any credible knowledge of alien contact or the role extraterrestrials play in creating crop circles. They are said to be interested in ball lightning. We would prefer to have them continue to believe it is a rare, natural phenomenon. Find out if they intend to conduct any other business here that we don't know about."

Charles Donovan replied, "We can do that" as he looked at Elise, who nodded.

"Charlie, you'll report to me on this," said Daniel. "Is there anything else we should cover today? I don't get to see you two very often."

Elise smiled and said, "Yes, we finished the photo editing job you gave us."

Daniel looked at Avery and said, "A year ago, someone discovered an R.A.F. file of reconnaissance photos taken in 1942 when they were updating the maps of England. The R.A.F. systematically photographed all of England. Recently, when an academic was reviewing the photographs as part of an agricultural research project, he discovered about fifty crop circles. He referred his findings to the Ministry of Defense. He thought the circles might have been navigational aids made by World War II German agents to guide bombers. The photographs then came to MI6, probably because nobody knew what to do with them. Elise, please explain what you did with the photographs."

Elise said, "Our MI6 photo analysts concluded that some were legitimate crop circles. We made a classified collection of those photos and removed them from the public R.A.F. files. The collection and report have been archived at MI6."

Daniel said to Avery, "We'll send a copy to your organization if you tell us where and how to send them."

"Fine," Avery replied. "I know some people who would like to have them." He thought, *The Dragonfly people will go crazy over these photos.*

CHAPTER 24

The Trip To Pewsey

As they exited customs at Heathrow, they heard a formal voice say, "Mr. And Mrs. Willard?"

Oh, no! Thought Dave. *What now?*

A tall, almost frail looking, very conservatively dressed middle-aged lady, with a full head of short cut gray hair appeared. She was wearing a light blue tailored suit and holding a wet umbrella. "Elise Witherton, Southern England Sacred Site Guide," she said. "Did you have a pleasant trip?"

In his foggy state, Dave recalled that this was the tour guide that Colson's travel agent had hired. "Willard, Dave Willard," said Dave.

"And I'm Raven, Ravi for short. Pleased to meet you, Ms. Witherton."

"Call me Elise. I'll be your guide while you're here. My home is near the bed and breakfast where you're staying. Your Colson travel agent didn't indicate your interests. I haven't arranged a structured tour for you. Here's a list of things most people like to see and do while they are here. I know all the locals and can arrange for you to meet with anyone in the crop circle community."

She handed a colorful travel brochure to Dave.

They loaded their bags onto a cart and chatted as she led them from the terminal to the parking area and her black SUV.

They drove in silence for a few minutes, until entering the M4 motorway. Ravi was in the passenger seat and Dave in the back, nodding off to sleep.

"How long will it take to get there?" asked Ravi.

"About an hour and a half," Elise answered. "In about forty-five minutes, we will turn off the M4 onto what you Americans might call a country road. Soon after that, we'll be in crop circle country."

As they drove, Ravi admired and commented on the countryside. Then Elise said, "Please tell me a little about yourselves so I can understand what you might like to see. I know you are from Los Angeles and that a Colson Associates travel agent made your travel arrangements. What kind of company is Colson?"

"It's a venture capital firm in Silicon Valley," Ravi replied. "But we're not associated with that part. Colson set up a scientific research nonprofit foundation which we work for."

"What kind of scientific research?" asked Elise, thinking, *This is going to be easy. She's volunteering answers to all the questions I'm supposed to ask.*

"Right now we're only sponsoring mathematicians doing theoretical research."

Elise turned to Ravi and said, "You don't look like a mathematician."

Ravi laughed. "No, I've degrees in education and English Lit. My husband is the scientific guy. We make a complementary pair. I bring a liberal arts viewpoint to our work."

Elise replied, "If your work here is scientific research on crop circles, I can put you in contact with people who have been involved with that." She then glanced at Ravi as she asked, "What are your personal interests?"

Ravi looked at Dave to see if he was still asleep and then answered, "I'm very interested in Metaphysics. I'd like to know what the local non-scientific people think is going on."

"We've lots of people in crop circle country who have non-scientific viewpoints," Elise answered. "There are many theories going around. I'll schedule some times to talk to people who have a variety of beliefs about who makes crop circles."

Ravi looked out the window at the scenery. The industrial-looking area around Heathrow had given way to woods, farmland, lakes, and occasional villages. "This is all so different from Southern California," She observed. "We don't have all this water, these green hills, lakes and streams."

Elise asked, "Where do you live in Los Angeles?"

"We live in a place called Playa Vista, near LAX, not far from the Pacific Ocean. We split our time between there and a place in the Mojave Desert."

"I don't know where the Mojave Desert is, exactly," Elise said politely."

It's north of L.A. over a range of mountains," Ravi answered "

"Why do you go there?"

"My husband inherited a cozy little house high on the side of a hill. When we don't have to be in L.A., we go there for the peace and quiet. We love the desert!"

Elise glanced at Ravi and asked, "What do you do there?"

"Dave does legal stuff, and I write."

"What do you write?"

"I'm working on a novel."

"What's it about?"

"A writer friend of mine says it's not a good idea to tell people about my work in progress. If I talk about it too much, I might not need to write it."

"I didn't mean to pry," Elise said quickly. She paused and then looked at Ravi. "Come to think of it, some people who come to crop circle country also spend a lot of time in the desert near someplace called Area 51. Is your desert home near there?"

Ravi thought for a second and then said, "I've heard of people going to some desert place to watch for flying saucers. I don't know exactly where that is. I know Dave wouldn't want to go there. He has no interest in UFOs."

Elise commented, "Okay, I won't try to hook you up with any of the locals who believe aliens are making the crop circles."

"Oh, no! Please don't do that," Ravi said. "We'd like to learn everyone's viewpoint about crop circles. Dave might like to hear what they say, especially about the balls of light. The scientist in him compels him to gather data before he forms conclusions."

"I can arrange to have you meet Charles Donovan," said Elise. "He is an old friend from my days working for the government. He's a very colorful gentleman, real British old-school."

Charles can find out what they know and what their real purpose is in coming her, she thought.

There was a long silence while Ravi looked out of the window. She then asked, "What job did you have in the government?"

"My late husband and I worked in developing foreign trade. We spent many years attached to foreign embassies promoting exports." She thought, *At least, that was the cover story.*

"How did you get from that to being a tour guide?" Ravi asked.

"When I attended university, I majored in anthropology. I was recruited to work on archeology digs out here during summer holidays. I met my late husband, a geologist, on one of those digs. We always loved this country and were fascinated with the local archeology. When we retired, we moved to a house not far from where you are staying. After my husband passed away two years ago, I had to find something to do, so I took up tour guiding."

"I'm sorry to hear of your loss," Ravi said gently.

Elise smiled and said, "I interred his ashes out here at one of his favorite places. I won't tell you where, but let me just say he has a really big gravestone, and I didn't pay for it."

Ravi laughed and said, "Is that a fringe benefit of being an archeologist?

"He would have approved of being interned there because the site has been thoroughly excavated and studied. Being there won't confuse any future archeologists."

Ravi yawned. "I'd like to hear more about him. Now, though, I need to crash for a while."

Elise said, "I understand. I've seen jet lag before."

Ravi laid her head against the window and was soon fast asleep.

They turned off the M4 and drove on a two-lane road for a few miles, and then Dave woke up, looked around and said, "Where are we?"

"We're about halfway there. We're nearing crop circle country."

The countryside glistened green in the late afternoon light. Seemingly endless wheat fields rolled to the horizon where puffy clouds marched, some dropping dark streaks of rain.

Ravi opened one eye, mumbled, "This is pretty country." and then went back to sleep.

Dave asked, "Is that wheat covering the hills?"

Elise answered, "Mostly, now. They grow different grain crops at other times of the year."

Dave was looking at the rolling wheat fields on each side of the road and observed, "Every fifty feet or so, there are tractor tracks going the length of the field. What are those for?"

Elise replied, "They have tractor rigs with long spray arms on both sides that go through the field spraying agricultural chemicals and fertilizers. Those tracks are convenient for walking into the fields to get to crop circles. You don't have to trample the wheat and make the farmers mad."

Ravi was awake again and asked, "Do the farmers like crop circles?"

"They don't like them. Ten or fifteen years ago, the crop circles were small, maybe twenty or thirty feet across. The farmers ignored them. In the past few years, the crop circles have been getting hundreds of feet wide. One circle can mash down thousands of dollars worth of wheat."

"I can see why the farmers might get mad," said Ravi.

Elise continued, "Some farmers put up donation collection boxes near their crop circles to make up for their loss. Lately, farmers have been erasing crop circles by mowing them out as soon as they are discovered to keep strangers from tramping through their property."

Dave asked, "When will we get to go to a crop circle?"

Elise answered, "You never know where you will find one. We'll stop if we see any. Tomorrow, I'll visit my local contacts that know where circles have recently appeared and make a plan to visit as many circles as you like."

"How do your contacts know where they are?" said Dave, picking up on the lingo.

"Two locals have ultralight airplanes, the little kind that looks like a hang glider and can use a driveway as an airport. They fly out every morning, spot new circles, and take pictures that local tourist shops sell. I can arrange for you to fly out in one of the ultralights."

No way, thought Dave. *That's a good way to end up dead!* "No thanks. I don't think our company insurance policy includes air travel by ultralight."

"Dave, what aspect of crop circles would you like to explore while you are here?" Elise asked.

"I've a scientific background and am interested in talking to people who are looking at them in scientific terms. I'm interested in the balls of light some people have observed."

Elise answered, "I know the gentlemen you can talk to about that." She thought, *That's a good piece of information to report to Donavan. I was beginning to think this pair was an ordinary couple of tourists.*

After a while, they passed through a small town. The main street was lined with red brick two story buildings, many of them painted, most probably hundreds of years old. They were set back from the street by narrow sidewalks, and sprouted windows hiding under second story rooftop dormers. Stone chimneys protruded from black slate roofs.

"We're only a few miles from the bed and breakfast where you will be staying. Sometimes there are crop circles within walking distance from there. I'll drop you off so you can check in, and leave you to rest until tomorrow. If you get hungry tonight, there is a pub, The Barge Inn, a fifteen minute walk from Kate's."

After a while, they turned up a drive from the main road and Elise said, "Here we are, at your bed and breakfast."

"It's cute," said Ravi. "It has a thatched roof on the old building in front."

Dave said, "It looks like it's an old farm house."

"No need to worry," said Elise. "You'll be staying in the modern addition. The owners live above the main room in the old building. The bottom floor was where the farm animals lived when the building was first built a couple of centuries ago. Now it is a modernized, communal breakfast and living room.

As they pulled up to the door, they saw a middle-aged, gray-haired lady in a loosely fitting, faded print dress working in the garden, Elise parked and introduced them.

"Welcome," said Kate. "Let me show you to your room."

CHAPTER 25

The Barge Inn

"I think we need to get something to eat," said Ravi yawning after a nap.

"I agree," Dave replied. "Kate said it's about a fifteen-minute walk to the Barge Inn, the only place to get something to eat. She said to walk on the dirt road through the wheat field to the canal, and then down the tow path to the inn."

"Good!" said Ravi. "I could use a good walk about now."

"Kate said it has good pub food and serves until eight."Dave looked at his watch. "We should probably get going."

As they walked along the dirt road through the wheat field, Ravi said, "This breathtakingly beautiful country. I love the light at this time of day on the rolling hills of green wheat. Kate told me sunset isn't until after nine o'clock. We should be back by then. She said that sometimes crop circles appear right in this field."

They came to the canal, a muddy stream about forty feet across, with a path along the bank, separating the canal from a lush green bramble of bushes and small trees. Narrow houseboats, about seven feet wide, with boxy cabins, were moored along the bank every few dozen feet. Each one displayed elaborate paint trimming in patterns of white, red, and blue.

They came to an ancient-looking two story sandstone colored building with bricks in differing colors, indicating that it had been rebuilt or added on to over the years. It sat adjacent to the tow path. The sign over the door read The Barge Inn.

"This looks like where we're having dinner," said Dave in a jovial tone.

The bar was hummed with men and a few ladies, apparently locals, noisily emptying mugs of beer, ale, or cider dispensed from a row of taps by a barkeep lady wearing jeans and a sweatshirt.

"Sit anywhere you want," said the lady, handing them menus between two of the revelers sitting at the bar.

Ravi and Dave went into the dining room and found an empty table across the room from a long table with about ten men and women noisily talking and draining mugs.

"The menu has the history of the inn on the back," said Ravi. She read it and then said, "This place was built about 1810 and has had many incarnations during the era the canal was busy with commercial and passenger traffic."

"I'm glad it's a restaurant now. I'm starved. Let's order," said Dave. "I must have fish and chips."

"Me too," added Ravi eagerly.

The barkeep came over and took their fish and chips orders and then said, "What will you have to drink?"

Dave asked, "What do you recommend from all those taps from behind the bar?"

"We've locally brewed Croppie and 1810 Ales, Area 51 and Pear Ciders, and our special Alien Abduction Green Beer. Three pints a day gives ninety-three percent protection from abduction. The green color makes you invisible to aliens.

"Do you have much trouble with abductions?" asked Dave with a straight face.

"A few years ago some boat people said they'd been abducted. Since we've been serving the Green Beer, we've had no problems."

Ravi said, "I'll try the Pear Cider. I've never had that. Does it offer protection?"

"The Inn management can't guarantee it."

"I'll try the Croppie Ale," said Dave. "What is a Croppie?"

"People like those over at that table who spend a lot of time investigating crop circles. Most of them are quite serious about it and have published books or sell pictures or stuff about crop circles."

The barkeep lady, writing on her order pad, walked away, and quickly returned with two mugs.

Ravi took a sip from her mug and said, "This is quite interesting."

Dave nodded his head in agreement as he drank.

As they sat, taking in the room, a short lady with long straight, obviously dyed, red hair, wearing a blue sweater and long printed skirt, came from the busy table, offered her hand to Ravi and said, "Hello, I'm Patty Deen. Are you here for the crop circles?"

Ravi shook her hand and said, "Yes we are. We just got here today. Are you one of the locals, a Croppie?" She paused with some embarrassment. "Is it okay to say that?"

"Yes. I've been here for six years investigating crop circles. I count myself as a Croppie."

"Have you written a book?" asked Dave as he thought, *I'd bet it's very scientific.*

"Yes, I've written three books. They're available from AMAZON and sold at the Well Bookfair in Avebury where all the tour busses stop."

"I'll look for them if we go there. What are the titles?" Ravi asked.

"The latest one is titled Crop Circles: Harbingers of Global Change."

Ravi pointed to a chair and said, "Would you like to join us? I'd like to hear about this."

Why does she have to do this? Dave thought. He smiled and said, "Please do. We're about to have another round. Will you join us?"

"Yes, thank you."

Dave waved, caught the bar lady's attention and pointed at all three mugs.

Patty needed no further prompting. "My books are about how people should prepare for the coming earth changes as predicted by the ancient texts of both the Eastern and the Western philosophies–prophets from the time of Nostradamus to the present and artifacts from ancient civilizations such as the Mayan Calendar. The signs are everywhere if we only look. We're nearing the time of change, the time when the earth goes through a wormhole into a new reality and the Earth's magnetic pole will shift. During the Earth's last trip through the wormhole, Atlantis disappeared."

Dave thought, I *don't think she got this theory from Stephen Hawkings or any of the other astrophysicists who base their thinking on logic.*

After the mugs had come, Ravi asked, "What's a wormhole?"

"Einstein and his theory of relativity and gravity shows us how there are black holes in space that suck everything into them. When the earth goes into one of these, it travels through a canal and emerges from the other side transformed. It's as though the Earth is going through a birth canal and is to be reborn."

Ravi was taking a notepad from her purse as Dave asked, "What do wormholes have to do with crop circles?"

"Crop circles pictographically tell us about the coming earth changes. The circles contain sacred geometry relationships that are a roadmap for our transition."

"When you say sacred geometry, do you mean the mathematical shapes that appear in nature such as spirals in snail shells?" asked Dave.

"Yes, they occur throughout the universe in shapes of spiral galaxies and other things. Interpreting crop circles will allow us to understand what we need to know to make this transition."

Ravi commented, "I don't know if I can ever understand about Relativity and Sacred Geometry. I'm not very scientific."

"You don't have to understand the science of it all. If you meditate in crop circles, the knowledge will come to you at a deeper level, a knowing."

The barkeep brought the fish and chips. Patty stood up and said, "It was nice talking to you. I give tours of crop circles and teach people how to meditate in them to decode their meaning. Here is my business card. I can arrange a private tour for you if you wish."

Ravi eagerly picked up the card as Dave said, "Thank you. We'll look for your books."

"My pleasure," said Patty as she picked up her mug of Croppie Ale, smiled, and left.

Ravi watched Patty return to the big table and then asked: "What do you think?"

Dave replied, "I'd like to look at some of her books before I decide. Colson sent us here to find about ball lightning." He thought, *This birth canal transition isn't what I remember from the Nova special that described black holes.* He then added, "Besides, we already have Elise as our guide."

Ravi said, "The menu said Fish and Chips; it should have said A Fish and Chips. Look, they served us each a foot-long whole fried fish on a bed of fries."

CHAPTER 26

A Crop Circle

"Kate, I love this!" gushed Ravi. "Is this called an English Country Breakfast?"

Kate smiled. "I guess you could call it that. We like to have our guests well fed before they start their busy days."

Dave said, "We like the thatched roof on this building. I was surprised they still use them. How long do they last?"

"Oh, my late husband had this one put on about twenty years ago. They're expensive but in keeping with the history of the building. I had it repaired a couple of years ago, and it cost. . ." She paused and then said, "about the equivalent of forty thousand U.S. dollars. When we built the annex you're staying in, we went for the tile roof."

Elise walked in wearing a brown tweed jacket and slacks tucked into her almost knee-high rubber boots. She sat down by the door and took off her boots.

"Do we need some of those?" Ravi asked.

Elise looked at Ravi and Dave's shoes and said, "I think what you have will be adequate. The wheat fields around here have a very sticky, chalk-like, gray clay soil. You may have to spend some time scraping your shoes off after we get back in the car from being in the fields. I have a scraper in my car.

"I just got finished talking to some of my contacts. There's a circle that appeared last night not far from here. We'll go there first."

Ravi said,"Oh, that's exciting!"

Dave added, "I'll finish eating so we can go.'

Elise answered, "Oh you Americans, always in a hurry! Take your time; it will be there for weeks. I need another cup of tea."

Kate disappeared into the kitchen and Elise sat down. "Let's talk about a plan for your visit. We'll see as many crop circles as possible. We'll visit Avebury, a village in the center of a large circle of standing stones that predate Stonehenge by a few hundred years. When the weather turns bad, we can visit with people who have been researching crop circles."

"That sounds good," said Dave. "Can we meet people who have looked at the scientific aspects of the balls of light?"

"Yes. I'll set up a visit with an old associate of mine who has an interest in them."

Ravi said, "Dave and I want to talk to people of all viewpoints: the scientific, the metaphysical, and those with supportable theories of who or what makes the circles."

Elise thought a second and then said, "The metaphysical is the easiest because we'll run into those people everywhere. I know a couple of men who have definite ideas of how crop circles are made.

"Now, let's get going. We have a circle to visit."

They drove down several country roads and then turned into a driveway with a locked gate. It appeared to be a farm machinery access to a large rolling wheat field. The field was scribed with the grid of straight tractor tracks.

Elise said, "We'll park here and walk to the crop circle. My instructions are to go left to the seventh set of tracks and then turn uphill. Those tracks will pass through the crop circle."

They got out of the car and put on small backpacks holding sweaters, water, and rain coats. They took turns holding the barbed wire fence wires apart as they climbed through.

They walked along the road next to the fence, then Elise said, "Here we are at seven. Let's go up this track." She led the way.

The wheat was waist high, bright green with spiked tops covered with green kernels.

Ravi said to Dave, "Isn't this neat, walking through the wheat in this bright yellow light? The plant energy is really good. Plants here must love all the rain they get."

Dave thought, *It's spectacular. But I don't know about plant energy.*

They walked about half a mile and then Elise stopped at a three-foot-wide track across the one they were following. "This is it," whispered Elise. "It looks like this cross-track is part of a big circle. I can see areas inside where the wheat is flattened. Walk around and figure out its shape."

"Aren't you going to guide us?" asked Ravi.

"I'd like to let you create your own experience. Walk, meditate, sleep, or do anything you want except alter the pattern. I have a book and will be sitting nearby reading. If you have questions or are ready to leave, come back here. Enjoy!"

Dave said to Ravi, "Let's walk this way around the circle."

After they had walked about a quarter of the way around the circle, Dave said, "It looks like the circle is about one-hundred fifty feet across and has a six-pointed star inscribed in it. The areas between the star and outer circle are flattened."

"Let's go into the flattened area and see what it feels like," said Ravi. They walked in, sat down, and then Ravi said, "I don't feel any different earth energy. In the Native American medicine circles to which my grandmother took me, I always felt a strong and special energy. Not here! I think I'll try my dowsing rods to measure the energy."

"I thought those rods were for finding water," said Dave. "I wondered why you were bringing them."

"They sense all manner of earth energy," said Ravi. "Watch and you will see."

Ravi, sat down and dug her dowsing rods from the backpack. They were two coat hanger wires, bent into an L shape that fit into Ravi's thumbs up fists and freely moved from side to side. As she walked around, she expected the wires to swing in different directions, unless they sensed something. Then they would point the same way. As Ravi walked through the circles, she did subtle dance steps and chanted under her breath. The rods never responded.

Dave yawned and said, "I'm still feeling a little jet-laggy. I think I'll lay down and close my eyes."

As Ravi walked around with her dowsing rods, she saw another guide and about ten high school-aged girls paused at the edge of the circle. The guide said, "We must stop and honor the circle. Ask its permission before you enter. While we are here, act reverently. Explore for awhile and then we'll get back together for a guided meditation." After the girls had spread throughout the circle, the guide saw Elise. She walked over to give her a hug, sat, and began to quietly talk.

Photo by Lucy Pringle copyright 2012

After her exploring, Ravi returned to where Dave was sleeping. She thought, *I'll lay down near Dave and meditate.*

Ravi woke to the sound of sobbing. She sat up, nudged Dave and said, "Do you hear that? It sounds like someone in trouble."

Dave stood up, looked around and said, "It's one of those teenage girls sitting in the next cleared section of the circle."

As they approached, a frail looking girl wearing a knit beanie hat over long blond hair looked up with runny mascara eyes.

Ravi asked, "Are you okay?"

"Oh yes, I was crying because the vision I had in my meditation was so wondrous and beautiful. I've never experienced anything like that before."

"We wanted to know if you were in distress. We'll leave you to your bliss." She took Dave's hand, and they began to walk to where Elise was sitting.

"Ready to go?" asked Elise.

"Yes," said Dave.

Ravi pointed to the other visitors. "Who are those teenage girls?"

"They're a tour group from the Netherlands. I've known their guide, Greta, for years. She brings several tours here every year and is known for powerful, directed meditations."

Ravi looked wide-eyed as she asked," Can you lead us in directed meditations?"

"No, I'm not trained in doing that," replied Elise. I've planned for us to visit a bookstore. You can buy Greta's book of meditations if it's in stock."

As they started walking down the tractor track toward the car, Ravi asked, "What were we supposed to experience in the circle?"

Elise smiled and said, "In my years of leading tours, I've learned not to coach people on what they should expect. I think people's beliefs and expectations have a lot to do with their response to being in a circle. Would you like to tell me what happened to you in the circle?"

Ravi answered, "I felt a strong plant energy from the wheat. It seemed to feel stronger in the circle than out here in the field." She looked at Dave.

"I felt something that pulled my awareness down toward a meditative state. I had a delightfully refreshing nap. It cleared my mind." Dave then thought, *When we entered the circle, my scientific skepticism had me in a judgmental mood evaluating whether the circle was a hoax or not. I don't feel that way now.*

Ravi thought, *We've no way to know what transpired with our unconscious minds while we were asleep.*

Then Dave volunteered, "The thing that impressed me most about that circle was the precision with which it was made. The curves were perfectly circular, and the straight lines exact. There were no fuzzy edges. It was like it had been cut by a laser. I was impressed by the craftsmanship and perfection of the layout."

Elise added, "Whoever or whatever makes the circles have to be both precise and fast. During this time of year, our nights are only about five hours long."

When they got back to the car, Elise said, "There's what you Americans might call a coffee shop and bookstore near here where some Croppies hang out. To be truthful, I have to say they mostly serve tea and marvelous biscuits. Shall we go?"

"Biscuits, oh boy," sang Ravi.

"Count me in," added Dave.

CHAPTER 27

Busted

I listened as HAL said, "This concludes our perceptual Earth mission 8-512, Mark I Crop Circle Creation and Observation. It has been a pleasure to have you aboard Mission 8-512 today. We hope you have had a pleasant mission and will travel with us again. Please check your seatbelt as we will experience some turbulence as we change dimensions. The pod door will open as soon as it is safe to disembark."

Things became a gray blur; a paralyzing vibration went through my bodysuit. I had the sensation of thunderous noise, then blackness, and then white and quiet. I heard the rotating machine slow down and felt it stop. I saw Dr. Ev press the green button, and the drawbridge extended to the pod.

The pod door opened as HAL said, "Please watch your step. Enjoy your visit here or at your final destination."

Dr. Ev frowned as best he could and said, "I think we have a problem!"

I had a feeling that you Earthlings might call "my heart sank," except our bodysuits have a circulatory system that does not require primitive heart pumps. *I don't understand,* I thought.

Everything went according to plan, and we collected a lot of data on suitable crop circle sites and earthling responses.

Dr. Ev continued, "You've received a violation ticket from the Earth Park Police. You interfered with Earth's history flow. Your student science project is at risk."

"I don't understand," I said. "I thought everything went well."

"You're supposed to report to the 356 Galaxy Park Police local office. They'll explain. Check your bodysuit into your locker. As you leave our laboratory, you will enter a reality the Park Police creates. After you finish with the Park Police, see Mr. Ob. He will tell you how you can proceed, if at all, on your student science project. Good luck! I hope you can continue."

He shook my hand, and I left. I checked in my bodysuit, walked out the laboratory door, and experienced a white flash. I was then wearing an earthling-like bodysuit, dressed in an orange garment, standing in front of the illusion of one of the earth buildings I had seen in my Knowledge Plate studies. In your terms, it was a red brick building, with two lamp posts in front, having large antique globes that bore the printed word, "Police." I walked up the granite steps and opened the glass doors labeled *356 Galaxy Earth Park Police.*

I strode to the desk and greeted the illusion of a severe looking earthling-like lady, wearing a black uniform, with a sewn-on Park Police patch. She looked up and growled, "What do you want?"

I felt intimidated as I said, "I was told to report here."

"What is your name?" she snapped.

"On Earth, I'm known as 'Mason.'"

She shuffled through some papers and then said, "Student Project License Violation?"

"Yes"

"Down the hall, second door to the left. Tell the bailiff you're there."

I was terrified as I walked through the door into what you would call a courtroom. I told the bailiff my name and he told me to take a seat and wait. As I sat, I noticed my orange jumpsuit had been stenciled to read, Park Police Detention.

Another apparent human being, dressed like me, in an orange jumpsuit, was being reprimanded by a scowling Judge in a black robe seated high above him behind a wide desk. The judge finished his tirade, banged a gavel on the desk and called, "Next!"

A droning voice said, "Mason, Student Experimental License violation: 'Disturbing Earthling's History Flow.' The license allows the student to visit 2000 sites on the earth between local dates of 1100 and 2100, in any place not excluded by other ongoing experiments, to produce patterns in crops, and to observe earthling reactions to those productions.

"Mason produced a circular pattern in a grain field near a village on the European continent in the time of 1276. The villagers reacted by accusing a local woman of witchcraft and burned her alive."

"That is not a violation of the experimental rules, as I read them," the Judge responded. He turned to a man dressed in a blue business suit sitting at another desk and said, "Dr. Oa, you are an expert in Earthling history, please explain."

Dr. Oa replied, "The student license is for creating isolated events and observing reactions. The student made a crop circle, and nearby villagers reacted by burning an accused witch. Although it's regrettable that an earthling died, it is acceptable as a response since it is a part of earthling social evolution. However, the student repeated the event by making seven more crop circles in the same area. That led to mass hysteria, burning of villages, a revolution, and the overthrow of a fiefdom king, which in turn changed the history flow of the region. The middle school student is not licensed to experiment with history flow. Those licenses are only awarded to postgraduates in appropriate majors."

The Judge scowled at me and said, "What do you have to say for yourself?"

I was intimidated as I replied, "Your honor, I was having trouble adjusting the experimental equipment. I did not know it made more than one circle. I made a thousand other isolated circles without incident."

The Judge turned to another man in a white lab coat and asked, "What do you think?"

He replied, "There may have been an equipment malfunction. I talked to Dr. Ev, the designer, and he said the experimental equipment has ben modified to prevent it from happening again."

The Judge looked at me and said, "We will not penalize you for this violation. However, I will rule that the space-time allocation of your license be modified to exclude highly superstitious eras and regions."

Dr. Oa added, "We recently granted a new graduate student license for an experiment called Aztec. We should also exclude that space-time from this student's license."

"So ordered!" said the Judge. "Anything else?" He looked around and then said, "Case dismissed with stated license modifications. Next!"

I walked from the courthouse, stunned, terrified. *Will this affect my grade or prevent me from continuing with my Earthlings courses?*

CHAPTER 28

The Science Guy

As they drove into the four-car gravel-surfaced parking lot, Dave thought, *This sure ain't no Starbucks.* The coffee house was a white flat-topped box with a serving counter and about ten stools. Two tables looked out onto the parking lot through plain, plate glass windows. Next to the coffee house was a one-car garage with an open door. A sign on the open door read *Book Store*.

"We're in Luck!" exclaimed Elise. I see Kerry Bratton's car here in the parking lot. He's one of the people who has been doing scientific research on crop circles. He is probably sitting on the patio in back. If we buy his book and ask him to sign it, he'll talk to us all day. Wait here and I'll find it for you."

In a minute, Elise returned with "The Agrarian Riddles" and handed it to Dave who sarcastically thought, *That's a great title.* He thumbed through the book and said, "It has lots of detailed photos and diagrams." He noticed that the cover was an aerial photo of an elaborate crop circle.

As they rounded the corner of the building to the covered patio, they saw a man sitting at a table reading, in deep concentration.

"Kerry!" called out Elise.

Kerry stood his muscular six-foot body up and left his chair to greet Elise with a broad smile and a two-armed handshake. "Jolly to see you again, Elise."

Elise made introductions and then said, "Dave and Ravi are here from America. Dave's interest in the scientific meaning of crop circles has led him to your book."

"Would you please sign it for me?" asked Dave.

"Please join me," said Kerry pointing to his table.

Elise picked up the teapot on the table and said, "I'll refresh this."

After he had inscribed the book, Kerry said, "Let me tell you how I became interested in crop circles. I'm a civil engineer. I used to design large buildings and so I appreciate how difficult it is to lay precise plots for foundations and structures. In 1991, I was on holiday up here and saw my first circle. I was amazed by the precision with which it was drawn in the field–not a single stalk of wheat in the wrong place– and intrigued by the design. When I first walked into the circle, I felt a strange emotion, almost a *deja vu* though I had never been in anything like that before. I had to know more about this phenomenon. Who made it? Why? Who was communicating with us and what was their message?"

Elise returned with two pots of tea and a plate of biscuits. "Oh boy!" said Ravi as she helped herself to a biscuit. "In the U.S., we call these cookies."

Dave studied Kerry a few moments and then asked, "Did you find any answers to your 'Who' and 'Why' questions?"

"Let me give you a short history. After World War II, people started to be very interested in UFOs. Sightings drew lots of news coverage. The idea of alien civilizations spying on us resonated with the public, and the media was delighted to jump on any story about UFOs. In 1965, an Australian farmer claimed he saw a flying saucer rise into the sky from a marshy lagoon, leaving behind a circular woven bed of reeds. The Australian Military investigated. World-wide media coverage resulted!

"In 1974, a Canadian farmer reported seeing a UFO and found a pattern of five crop circles. Canadian Mounties concluded that they were not a hoax. Around that time, there were many UFO sightings in Canada. More worldwide media coverage!"

"I didn't know crop circles have shown up in Canada," Dave commented.

Kerry laughed and said, "Crop circles have appeared in more than 50 countries, in almost every country where they grow grain crops. But, back to my story.

"In England, crop circles thirty to fifty-feet in diameter had been observed by farmers in this area since before 1945. Farmers didn't pay much attention to them. They attributed the circles to whirlwinds or other natural phenomena. When the idea of crop circles became associated with UFOs, visitors came to try to see flying saucers. Aliens became the 'Who' causing crop circles. The UFO drive motors or landing gear were believed to have caused the flattened circles.

"In 1991, after this area had attracted a lot of UFO attention two locals, Dave and Doug, claimed that they had made all of the crop circles that had appeared since 1978. They demonstrated how to use boards held to their feet by ropes to stomp out crop circles. The 'Who' became Dave and Doug, and the 'Why' became to play a trick on all the UFO believers. The media ate up the story. The news that crop circles were all a hoax resulted in world-wide coverage!"

"Before I started my current investigation of crop circles I thought that they were all a hoax," Dave admitted. I guess people are quite willing to accept 'hoax' as a simple explanation for things they don't understand."

Kerry leaned forward. "I agree. Soon after crop circles were labeled hoaxes, as if in rebuttal, enormous, complicated crop circles began to appear. The 'Who' became 'an unknown intelligence" and the 'Why' became 'communicate an esoteric message to humanity.'

"This is where I came into the story. My engineering background led me to conduct scientific measurements. Analysis of the patterns revealed mathematical relationships that could only be known by well-educated higher intelligences. We found Fibonacci numbers in the geometric ratios measured. These are the same numbers we find in biological settings, such as branching in trees, the arrangement of leaves on a stem, the fruit sprouts of a pineapple, the flowering of an artichoke, and uncurling of a fern.

"We found crop circles aligned along logarithmic spirals and the shapes of sacred geometry that are the basis for the design of temples of Egypt, Greece, Rome, and cathedrals of Medieval Europe. One circle, when decoded, yielded the number of pi to ten significant figures."

Ravi said, "In my studies in Art History, I've seen reference to sacred geometry as arrangements of shapes of buildings that are most pleasing to the human eye. What does that have to do with crop circles?"

Kerry paused and then said, "It means that some intelligence is skillfully making the crop circles here and in over 50 countries, often at the same time, exhibiting complexity and intelligence. The crop circles are made with precision and speed that is beyond human capability."

Ravi asked, "Do you mean all circles are from some unknown origin?"

Kerry replied, "No, there are hoaxes but serious investigators can spot them. It is analogous to how experienced jewelers can tell real diamonds from cubic zirconium fakes. To an experienced eye, real circles are much different from man-made. For instance, real circles look precisely drawn. Hoaxes are often ragged or sloppily laid out."

"What evidence is there extraterrestrials make crop circles?" asked Dave as he thought, *I've got to hear this.*

Kerry seemed proud to have the answer. "In 1974 the Search for Extra Terrestrial Intelligence (SETI) program transmitted a message from an enormous antenna in Puerto Rico with the hope that other planetary intelligence might receive it. The message was a graphic that showed Earth's location and some key things about humans and our planet. In 2001, we received a reply!"

Elise began to worry as she thought, *This discussion is going the wrong way.*

Kerry continued, "A crop circle in the format of the SETI graphic sent in the 1974 transmission appeared as an answer. The graphic showed the location of the senders and some of their body characteristics. A year later another formation appeared with a portrait of a space being. We all anxiously await our next communication."

Elise thought, *My instructions from MI6 are to keep them away from people who might talk about extraterrestrial intelligence.*

Dave was about to ask a question when Elise looked at her watch, interrupted Kerry's talk and politely said, "Thanks, Kerry. We appreciate your time. Now, I think I have to get back on schedule and take our visitors off to another circle."

Dave said, "Thank you, Kerry. I will read your book with great interest." He thought, *I'm not convinced.*

CHAPTER 29

The Second Circle

They parked in a two-car parking lot near an open pedestrian gate and a path leading into a wheat field. A computer printed sign read "To the Crop Circle." They walked through the gate and saw another sign with an arrow directing them along the base of the hill. A sign on a locked wooden box read, "Suggested Donation: 2 pounds per person." Dave dropped six pounds in the box as he said, "They charge admission?"

Elise explained, "Some farmers feel they should be compensated for crop damage. He probably put up the direction signs so that visitors don't go stomping all over the field hunting for the circle."

After walking about a quarter mile, they saw another printed sign directing them to a pair of tractor tracks that went up the hill. As they climbed through the waist-high wheat, Dave said, "This is beautiful! This track goes uphill and disappears over the horizon. This field spreads like a giant wave stretching miles on each side."

Ravi intoned, ". . . and feel the plant energy."

In the distance, on a hill above them, they saw five people walk across the field and turn onto the tractor track.

Elise said, "They must be coming from the circle."

As they passed, they smiled and said a greeting in a language Dave didn't understand. Elise greeted them in the same language and talked one of the men in the group. As the visitors walked down the hill, Elise said, "That group was from Finland. He told me about two other circles to visit. I think we turn here to get to this circle."

They walked a few feet and then entered a circle about fifteen feet across. Elise pulled her book from her bag and said, The man I talked to said this pattern is circles joined by curving paths. I'll wait here until you're ready to go."

Ravi pointed to a tuft of wheat intricately wrapped into a spike in the center of the circle and asked, "What is that?"

Elise looked. "That is one of the hallmarks of many circles. Examine it and you'll see it has wheat stocks in layers wound in opposite directions. There are many theories as to how those are made, whirlwinds, flying saucer magnetism, ball lightning, and so forth. I'll let you figure it out." She spread her jacket on the ground and sat. "I'll be right here."

Ravi and Dave walked about twenty steps along a path and then came upon a circle twice the diameter of the first. Dave looked around and then said, "It looks like there is one big circle connected by curving paths to five smaller ones."

Dave visited each of the circles, and with his usual scientific observation skills noted their precision. In one circle, he felt under the center tuft to see if a pole had been stuck in the ground for mapping out the circle. There was no trace.

When they met up back in the largest circle, Ravi said, "I didn't find any unusual energies with my dowsing rods."

"These circles and paths are not as precisely cut as the last circle," Dave observed.

A teenaged boy, wearing jeans, a bulky brown jacket, and rubber boots, said, "Would you like a picture?" He picked up a long aluminum pole, like those used by window washers, with a camera mounted on the end. He looked Ravi and Dave over and then said, "Ten pounds. I'll email the pictures to you. The camera will show you and the entire circle."

"Okay." Dave said agreeably, then asked, "Is this your family's farm?"

"Yes," the boy replied. "I do this to save for my education."

"How long has this circle been here?"

"Eight days. It's getting a little trampled."

"Do you often get circles on this hill?"

"Usually, we have two in the summer. Never in the same place."

As the boy took Dave's email address and ten-pound note, Dave asked. "Do you ever see who or what makes them?"

The boy looked down at his boots and said, "No, they appear over night. Joe Dedder, the pilot of one of the ultralights, calls my dad when he spots one on our farm. I have to go now. I'll email you the pictures tonight."

"Seems like a nice kid," said Ravi.

"He didn't want to talk about who made the circles." observed Dave.

They joined Elise, who was standing looking at the view. "I don't see any more circles. We should stop by another bookstore and have lunch. There are usually some croppies there.

This bookstore was a house, sitting near the street, bearing a roughly lettered sign that read Crop Circle Information. Elise parked in the empty lot next door. "Look around the bookstore and then go around to the back to the snack bar, order your lunch, and pick out a picnic table. I'll talk to some people inside about where the circles are. I'll see whom I can find for you to talk to."

After browsing in the bookstore and buying several books, they ordered their lunch. After they had been seated at a table, Ravi took a big bite out of her sandwich and said, "I've never tasted Interstellar Ham before."

Dave replied, "I'll bet it's not as good as my Abduction Special."

Elise came out of the building, carrying sandwiches, accompanied by a grandfatherly-looking, short man. They sat down, and she said, this is "Benny Chastain. He has had experience with the ball lightning."

"That I have," said Benny with some pride.

"Have you been close to ball lightning?" Dave asked.

Benny began, " I've seen it many times from a distance. One night, I had a close encounter. Some of us were camped out on a hill from which we could see several fields where crop circles would form. A storm blew in, and we hid in our tents during torrential rain and lightning. As it was getting light, we saw a new circle. We ran down to the circle and saw that there was a ball of lightning floating around."

"How big was it?" asked Dave.

"It was about three feet in diameter with an inner orange glow. Even though there was no wind to move it, the ball floated around about four feet over the circle. I was terrified as it came toward me. When it was five feet in front of me, it moved up, flew over my head and continued on its way."

Dave was intrigued as he asked, "Was it hot? Did you smell anything? Did it make any noise?"

"I didn't sense anything. It bobbed up to avoid me and went on its way. It stopped glowing and disappeared a minute later."

"Do you have any idea what it was doing?"

"No. I think it has something to do with those black helicopters we see around crop circles. One of my friends saw one of those helicopters hover above a circle while commandos slid down ropes. Sometimes we see lights in the sky at night and think it might be ball lightning, but it just turns out to be a black helicopter doing whatever it is they do. I don't think the helicopters make circles, but they appear near them. Many times they have a photographer hanging out taking pictures of the people visiting a circle. I'd like to know–why are the helicopter people keeping track of us? One thing I'm sure of, the government is up to something with crop circles."

Elise thought, *This is good. He's muddying up the water with one of the conspiracy theories he is known for.*

"Have you had other encounters?" Dave asked.

Benny smiled and said, "Yes. One time, when I was but a kid, my brother and I were playing in the loft of a neighbor's barn because there was a thunderous storm brewing. A ball of lightning came through the closed barn door below us. It floated around for awhile and then went out through a side wall. We hid for awhile and then investigated. It didn't leave any trace, a burn mark or anything, as it went through the door and wall."

Ravi inquired, "Weren't you scared?"

"Very. We would have been in trouble if we'd told anyone we'd been in the barn. My father had forbidden us to play in the neighbor's barn. If he'd found out about us risking our lives by being near the ball lightning, there would have been the devil to pay. When he was a young man, he saw ball lightning catch a haystack on fire and then explode."

"Have you had any other encounters?" asked Dave.

"My mates and I have seen the balls over fields about ten times. One time it was over a new crop circle. That's all."

Ravi said, "Back to crop circles. How long have you known them to appear around here?"

Benny thought for a second. "Oh, way back to the days when Doug and Dave were making them. Maybe earlier, I don't quite remember."

Elise thought, *Uh! Oh! We're getting too close to revealing classified data.* She recalled the World War II R.A.F. aerial photographs of crop circles that she had edited and classified.

To change the subject, Elise asked demurely, "Benny, I hear there's a new circle above Kennet Avenue near Avebury. Do you know anything about it?"

Benny thought for a minute and then said, "I don't think so."

Elise rose and said, "Thank you very much, Benny, I nee to get my visitors off to another site."

As they were saying goodbye, Benny gave Dave his business card and said, "I *also* give tours."

CHAPTER 30

Avebury

"Avebury is a Neolithic site, a village located in the center of three large stone circles, surrounded by a trench about thirty feet deep. It dates from about 2600 BCE," Elise informed them as they neared the town.

In the cultivated field on one side of the roadway, two rows of megalithic stones run parallel to the country road leading into Avebury.

Elise stopped the car near one of the stones about a quarter mile from the village. "Here we are. One of the newest circles is up that hill and over to the right."

They worked their way through a barbed wire fence into a pasture of cows, past the rows of stones and to another fence separating a hillside covered with wheat. They walked up a tractor track toward the crest of the hill.

Ravi looked around and exclaimed, "This is beautiful! I wonder how they got all of those stones here? They must be fifteen feet tall and go on for a mile."

"Must have had cheap labor," Dave said with a laugh.

After about half a mile, they came to the crest of the hill and followed another track to the right another half mile. Ahead they saw people in the circle. As they entered the formation, Elise sat down, reached into her pack for her book, and said, "I'll wait for you here."

"Look at the view!" marveled Ravi. "Miles and miles of wheat fields interrupted by pastures filled with cows."

Dave examined the crop circle pattern in the grain. "It looks like it is a pyramid shape about a hundred feet across with the tip pointing toward the top of the hill."

Ravi added, "There are one, two . . . six rows of smaller pyramids inside the big pyramid."

As they walked around, Dave said, "Look how precisely all the lines are drawn, and how sharply the edges are cut."

Ravi said, "A group of people is gathering in that corner. Let's see what that is all about."

An attractive lady, about thirty years old, was gathering her tour group around her. Everyone sat. She looked at Ravi and Dave for a few seconds and then smiled and nodded her head. "You're welcome to join us. I'm going to be channeling a message about the crop circle."

Ravi and Dave seated themselves behind the other people. The lady doing the channeling bowed her head in meditation. After about two minutes of silence, the channel raised her head, eyes closed and said, "I bring you greetings on this beautiful day in this crop circle.

"As you have seen on our tour, crop circles express many ideas. People gave you a variety of explanations as to why circles are here and what they communicate. Let us give you another idea. Crop circles are an avenue of energy, erupting out of the unconscious mind of humanity–of all of humanity–from what some would say is the collective unconscious mind which wants to communicate with the conscious world."

The lady paused as though she was listening to the source of information. Then she spoke again.

"Photo by Lucy Pringle copyright 2012

In a volcano, the lava flows from its weakest crack. In this part of the world, there is a crack where that eruption of consciousness comes through. The message seeping from these circles is that there's something bigger than you, an intelligence that can create. It's creating an abstract message from the soul in its language of pictures and imagination. It says, 'The Goddess is returning, and before she returns, you need to learn her language of imagination, the language of pictures.'"

Dave thought, *A few days ago I would have thought this was all a bunch of garbage. But now this is all starting to make sense. Maybe something is seeping into my consciousness during my exposure to crop circles?*

The channel continued, "You should not come here to look at the circles and admire their creativity or craftsmanship. You should experience them with your whole self. Look at them. Sense what your emotions and intuition are saying. Use your hands to feel the energies of the grain growing inside and outside of our of the circle. Do deep meditations in the circles. Experience the depth of the meaning.

"When you were children learning to read, you had to learn the alphabet and then move up to the elementary readers like Run Dog Run. Here, you start with the literature of the Soul. It will come to you if you listen to it hard enough."

Dave thought, *the literature of the soul? I feel that I know what that means. It makes sense. But how do I know that?*

Then the channel grew quiet and bowed her head for a minute. Everyone was silent. She raised her head, looked around blurry eyed, and smiled. Everyone applauded quietly.

Ravi was pensive as they walked away. She said, "That was quite an experience!"

Dave thought, *Channeling? What's next?*

They found Elise and walked along the tractor track at the crest of the hill.

Dave grew very thoughtful as he looked around. *Over there, I see Silbury Hill, a 150 foot or so high mound constructed a couple of thousand years ago, I see the stones leading to the henge and rows of stones circling Avebury. Whatever is 'easing through the cracks' has done so a long time here.* Then abruptly he thought, *Is something else going on here?*

CHAPTER 31

Mason Reports

Mr. Ob joined me in my illusion atop a desert hill overlooking a village of crumbling battle-scarred white buildings. Armored tanks and rocket launchers bearing black flags decorated with Arabic symbols lurked behind a wall. Soldiers held up their rapid-firing assault weapons and shot toward the town. The chatter of machine guns was interrupted by the sound of the artillery shelling of any building still standing. In the village, soldiers scampered from building to building or returned fire from behind the rubble.

"What's going on?" asked Mr. Ob.

"It's a war between two hostile tribes of Earthlings that has been fought for centuries. The tribes have forgotten why they started hating each other. Now, it is about seeking revenge against one another for atrocities they take turns committing. I'll move the illusion to a peaceful place."

We were suddenly dressed in loose-fitting white robes, sitting in the shade of a grove of palm trees surrounding a watering trough and a well.

Mr. Ob looked surprised. "Good choice of illusions! I've never seen this warring kind of Earthling behavior. Now, what is this peaceful place?"

"Earthlings call this a 'desert oasis,'" I said.

We were quiet for a while and then Mr. Ob broke the silence and said, "I heard you got in trouble with the Earth Park Police. Dr. Ev said that it might have been an equipment malfunction. Not your fault. It won't effect your Earthlings course grade."

"I'm relieved to hear that. I wanted to check with you about my plans for a new series of crop circles. I'm worried that I'll interfere with Earthling history flow."

I went on to explain to Mr. Ob, "In my project, I first spread simple circles through what Earthlings perceive as time and space. None of the Earthlings paid much attention for hundreds of years until something made them believe my patterns in grains were made by alien flying saucers. Then, Earthlings began making circles that looked like mine. It then became a secret art form where artists made large, elaborate patterns during the night. Earthlings believed the circles were esoteric messages to humanity authored by alien civilizations, the spiritual energy of the earth, or various other sources."

Mr. Ob smiled and said, "That is an excellent Middle School Science Project result. That should get you a high grade from the elders."

I was hesitant to add, "I would like to make circle authorship a continuing mystery. Sooner or later, Earthlings may decide that Earthlings make most of the circles. Dr. Ev has a new generation device capable of making large, complicated patterns embodying relationships that are understood by the earthling priesthood they call mathematicians. I want to see how they answer the question, 'If Earthlings didn't make the patterns, who did, and why.?'"

Mr. Ob hesitated and then said, "That sounds like a fruitful addition to your student project plan. Why are you concerned?"

"I plan to spread these throughout the illusion they call time. The Park Police judge said I must avoid times and places where Earthlings are superstitious. I will start making patterns at the beginning of the era when Earthlings got excited about flying saucers. Here is my question: Is it 'disturbing history flow' for me to change the history of circles by placing complicated patterns in the time dimension that would be earlier than the simple patterns I've already placed? It might alter the evolution of the Earthling-made circles."

"I don't think so," said Mr. Ob. "Earth reality is such that Earthlings will conclude that the complicated patterns were always there. It won't change the larger history context."

"Oh! Thank you," I said.

He replied, "It's always a pleasure to visit with you and share these remarkable Earth illusions you create."

We exited the oasis illusion. Then, I created an artillery shell that blew it up.

CHAPTER 32

Elise Reports

Elise used her MI6-issued secure cell phone to call Charles Donovan. "Hello, Charlie. It's beautiful in the countryside this time of year." (That greeting was the coded verification that it was Elise calling on official business.)

Charlie answered, "How is it in Scotland?"

"Warm for this time of year," Elise replied, and thought, *It's okay to talk business now.*

Charlie asked, "How is your tour group doing?"

"They're having a good time. I've only shown them circles made by the people we know. They've talked to croppies with metaphysical beliefs. Kerry Bratton gave him the scientific viewpoint. When he started to talk about Extra Terrestrial Intelligence, I managed to steer him off the subject. It's supposed to rain tomorrow. I'd like to drive the Willards over to Glastonbury and speak with you about black helicopters and other things you were involved with when you were attached to the military near here."

Charlie replied, "I'll be happy to talk to them. Let's meet at my Glastonbury office. You know where it is."

CHAPTER 33

Glastonbury

"We borrowed an umbrella from Katie," said Ravi as she opened the door of Elise's car. "Did you have breakfast? Is it supposed to rain all day?"

Elise replied. "I had something at home before I left. The weather report predicts hard rain. This will be a good day to visit one of my friends, Charles Donovan, in Glastonbury. When he worked for the government, he was attached to the military command that has training sites around here. He can tell us about the black helicopters and other things you've heard about."

Dave was brushing the rain off his jacket as he added, "I'll look forward to it. Benny Chastain seemed to believe that the military and their black helicopters were somehow involved in crop circles. I'll be glad to hear what the military command does."

Elise responded with, "Charlie is a very reliable source. He was a great friend of my husband's. You Americans might call him a 'straight shooter.'"

"My kinda guy," said Dave. "What else is in Glastonbury?"

"The Glastonbury Abbey is a ruin that dates to around two thousand years ago. Jesus's uncle built the original Abbey, the first Christian church. It has been rebuilt many times."

"I read a little about Glastonbury," said Ravi. "Isn't it supposed to be the Avalon of the legends of King Arthur?"

"Before the Romans drained the marshland, the Glastonbury hill was an island. About five hundred years ago, they dug up a coffin near the Abbey containing remains claimed to be those of King Arthur and Guinevere. That fed the belief that Glastonbury was the mythical Avalon."

"Will we have time to visit the Abbey?" asked Ravi.

"Yes, we can talk with Charlie as long as you like. Then you can explore the Abbey. Let's hope the rain lets up."

"Why is it in ruins?" asked Dave. "Other cathedrals dating from the 16th century aren't in ruins."

"It was abandoned to decay after 1539 when King Henry VIII dissolved the Catholic Church and created his Church of England. He wanted to divorce his wife and the Catholic Church wouldn't let him. So, he created his own church that would allow his divorce."

That was convenient, thought Dave.

"When he decided to dissolve the Catholic Church the Abbey was the target of his first takeover. It was powerful and had great stores of gold from owning the productive farmland in the surrounding area. After the takeover, the Abbey was closed, and its assets sold off to nobility and big landowners.

"That's about all the history I can remember. The visitor's center has displays that can show you more."

It was quiet for awhile, and then Ravi jokingly asked, "Are we almost there, yet?"

"Coming up on Glastonbury," said Elise with a smile. "Charlie's office is here in the newer area of town."

They parked and climbed a flight of stairs to a door with a small plaque that read, "Charles Donovan Holdings."

"Welcome!" said Charlie as he extended a hand to Dave then Ravi and then Elise. "Visitors from America–how jolly that you could stop by. Please have a seat."

The office had a dark oak desk, three guest chairs, a bookcase filled with photos of Charlie and friends, military memorabilia, and a very substantial looking safe.

"How are Alice and the boys?" asked Elise.

"They're all doing fine. My youngest is at Oxford. Ben is working for the government."

He turned to Dave and Ravi and said, "My wife made me take this office to get me out of the house. After so many years of me being away on government business, she can't stand to have me at home all day."

After a few minutes of more pleasantries, Charlie asked, "Why are you interested in crop circles?"

Dave replied, "We work for the Colson Foundation, a non-profit, scientific research foundation. He became curious about crop circles after he saw them from an airplane on approach to Heathrow. His curiosity was piqued when he talked to a friend here in England an heard ball lightning appears around crop circles."

Elise looked at Charlie. "You were involved in investigations into circles when you worked with the military. Kerry Bratton said that the government and their black helicopters have something to do with crop circles."

Charlie laughed and said, "In the area around Wiltshire, the military has several bases where they train special forces troops. They train in black helicopters for night missions.

Charlie pointed toward a black model helicopter in his bookcase of memorabilia. "That's like one of the ones they use in training.

"When they began training in the area around Wiltshire they discovered crop circles. Curious pilots and crews would fly around looking at them.

"The locals complained about the helicopters. A member of Parliament demanded an explanation of the black helicopter activity. We couldn't say the pilots were acting like tourists. The pilots were ordered to avoid crop circles."

"I can understand that," Ravi said, Simple curiosity on behalf of the pilots became 'government conspiracy.' I can see how some of the people we've talked to would jump on the idea of a conspiracy."

"The Ministry of Defense became interested in crop circles when reports of encounters with ball lightning started coming in. The M.O.D. sent some boffins out to investigate."

"Boffins?" asked Ravi. "What are they?"

Charlie thought for a second and then said, "I guess Americans would call Boffins science geeks or maybe scientists."

"What did they find?" asked Dave.

"They concluded that ball lightning is an inexplicable product of lightning storms. It floats around randomly and then disappears."

Dave asked, "Did the pilots observe anyone making circles in the night?"

"Yes," Charlie answered. "Their night vision equipment allowed them to see some of the circles being made by people. They've never seen any aliens making them."

Elise interrupted, "They are going to talk to one of the professional circle artists tomorrow. It won't upset them if you tell them what the pilots saw."

"On occasions," Charlie continued, "the pilots saw crews of about five people making patterns with boards and lawn rollers. The helicopter crews were ordered not to talk about seeing the circle makers. The circles are such big tourist attractions. Many people's livelihoods depends on visitors coming to see the crop circles. It would be politically unwise for the Ministry of Defense to announce anything derogatory about crop circles."

"Tell them about the fiasco people at the Radio Astronomy site almost created," Elise prompted.

"Elise told me it is safe to relate this in confidence. It's still officially classified. Can I be assured you will not divulge this to others?"

Dave looked at Ravi, who nodded. "Yes, I'm a lawyer. I'll treat this information as privileged. You have my word."

Charlie continued, "At one time the M.O.D had a small detachment doing some classified work at the radio astronomy facility. They were separate from the radio astronomy group. They had a lot of extra time on their hands. A couple of the enlisted men wanted to play a joke on the Croppies. They decided to inscribe a fake message from aliens in a wheat field and see what would happen. The enlisted men worked unobserved during daylight for several days to create an elaborate 'message from the aliens.'"

Elise said to Charlie, "They've heard about this formation from Kerry Bratton. He showed them a picture of the message and told them about the importance of the alien communication."

Charlie continued, "After the message was 'discovered,' the local experts came out to investigate. They were ecstatic. The pattern was proof that aliens were communicating to us through crop circles."

"The M.O.D. was again concerned about the public relations nightmare that would result from the public finding out that military people at a secret facility had made the pattern. We classified the information of the government's involvement. Nobody at the facility could talk about it without fear of going to prison.

"The last I heard, the young men who made the patterns were finishing their enlistment in the tribal area of Afghanistan.

Elise added, "The secret of who made the pattern has held up for over a decade. I believe that if the secret did get out, few of the locals would want to believe it."

There was a pause and then Elise asked, "Any further questions? We should get on to the Abbey soon."

Dave said, "No. Charlie, I would like to thank you for your time. I'm glad we won't go home with any misinformation about black helicopters and alien messages." He thought, *This guy would make a very credible witness in a trial.*

✻✻✻✻✻✻

As Elise dropped them off in downtown Glastonbury, she said, "I'll give you some free time to have lunch and visit the Abbey. You also may like to explore the local shops. I'll visit my favorite bookstore. We'll meet again at three o'clock in that coffee shop across the street from here."

It was raining hard. They found a restaurant, ate, and then visited a couple of New Age shops. Ravi said, "These shops look like the ones we have in LA. Let's brave the rain and walk down to the Abbey."

Inside the Abbey, they explored the museum that delineated the history of the Abbey and showed models of the buildings.

"It looks like the rain is letting up." Dave picked up the umbrella. "Let's go outside."

"These ruins are truly ruins," observed Ravi as they walked around. "In the museum, I read that after Henry VIII had sold off the property, the ruins became an urban quarry. Locals hauled off the finished stones and used them to construct other buildings. The only things now standing are a few high walls and arches that weren't worth taking apart."

Dave said, "If you've seen one ruin, you've seen them all. It's raining harder. Let's go back inside."

"Wait!"Ravi pleaded, "Let's see King Arthur's burial place. Please!"

"Okay, answered Dave. "But I'm getting awfully wet out here."

They found the burial plot, read the plaque marking the grave, and then Dave pleaded, "Let's find someplace to get out of the rain."

Ravi said, "Look over there. People are going into that building. Let's hurry!"

They went inside and saw that a large group of tourists was seated, listening to a monk in a brown, hooded, rough textured robe. He was speaking in German as he pointed out the various features of the vaulted ceiling room.

The monk finished his talk. Everyone applauded. The tour guide stood, said something in German, and the whole audience filed out the door.

Dave said, "Let's sit here awhile and take in the room."

"Maybe the rain will let up," added Ravi.

The other visitors left.

The monk came over to them and said, "Hello, I'm Brother Paul. I noticed you when you came in. Do you understand German?"

Dave said, "No," as Ravi shook her head.

"Where are you from?" asked Brother Paul with an educated British accent.

Ravi answered, "Los Angeles. We're here to investigate crop circles. What does the Church think about crop circles?"

"I'm not a monk. My real name is Paul Hanson. I'm a docent in the living history program. The Abbey hasn't been part of the Catholic church since 1539 when Henry VIII dissolved the Church. Most of the year I'm a historian in the Glastonbury History Library. On weekends, I put on this costume and pretend it's the fourteenth century.

"What is this building?" asked Ravi.

"This is the fourteenth century Abbot's kitchen. The Abbey hosted many visitors, and they had to feed hundreds of people at every meal."

"I can see it was quite an operation," commented Dave.

Brother Paul gave a short lecture on the Abbey's history and then said, "You're investigating crop circles. We hear a lot about them over here. What have you observed?"

Dave replied, "We've only just begun our investigation. People have a lot of firmly held beliefs about them."

Brother Paul thought for a second and then said, "As a historian I have to think that's normal. People acquire sets of beliefs and then create their life around those beliefs. In Glastonbury, we have neo-Pagans who create the reality that they are living in mythical Arthurian times.

"We saw some of them in the restaurant," Ravi said. "They dressed in Medieval clothes and spoke in a lingo of that era."

Brother Paul continued, "Some locals believe Glastonbury was the mythical Avalon and that the real Arthur is in the grave in the Abbey. That is their reality. Historians now believe that the Arthur only existed as an ancient myth, and that the Tomb of Arthur was a twelfth-century creation of some Abbey monks to promote visitation.

Dave pondered a minute and then said, "In our investigation of crop circles, we've run into many–firmly held beliefs–about crop circles and what they mean. Nobody can prove their idea is right or that the others are wrong.

"Since we are here in the Abbot's kitchen, allow me to use a food metaphor," said Brother Paul. "People seem to search for ideas which appeal to them and *cook* them into their *belief stew*. Then, they ignore anything that that isn't made from their own recipe. History is rife with true-believers who will only eat from their own stew."

Belief stew. I'l have to remember that for my book, Thought Ravi

Dave paused for a minute and then said, "When we first came here, I was very judgmental. I had the arrogant idea that the people who believed in crop circles were being conned. There was no scientific explanation for why they exist. I was only willing to add approved ingredients to my belief stew.

"We have sampled many people's beliefs about crop circles. Who am I to judge who has the true recipe?"

Ravi thought, *Wow! This attitude is a delightful change. Before we came here, I was afraid he might pull his drawbridge up and not let any non-scientific ideas in. This is the man I love, the one that can listen and be open to new ideas.*

Dave continued, "Since the have been here I have realized that before one swallows any true belief, it is good to salt it with a few good shakes of doubt."

Brother Paul nodded his head in agreement and said, "That's one of the lessons of History."

CHAPTER 34

Mason's Third Flight

I entered the Vehicle Laboratory wearing my bodysuit, and greeted Dr. Ev. He smiled a little smile which was as much as he could do with his bodysuit and said, "I have HAL 8.6 ready to go. Instead of only inscribing simple circles, you'll now be to make complicated patterns with a drafting machine. One pattern I've programmed has over three hundred small circles. HAL will show you the changes in operation. Ready to go?"

"Yes," I said, even though it was difficult to make the "Y" sound with this bodysuit.

I climbed the steps and crossed the bridge to the pod. I got in and placed my hands and feet on the control surfaces. I gave a thumbs up to Dr. Ev, who had walked back to the control console. He waved and pressed a red button. I heard a familiar voice.

HAL droned, "Greetings, Mason, and welcome aboard Earth mission 8-514, Advanced Crop Circle Creation. Please keep your seatbelt fastened at all times because we may experience field disturbances. I'll be your pilot today as we perceptually travel to Earth. After the triple rotator reaches speed, you'll experience a moment of no perceptions, and then we'll be at your destination."

The machine began to rotate, then speed up and tumble. A paralyzing vibration went through my bodysuit, followed by thunderous noise and blackness. Then, white and quiet.

HAL said, "We've arrived at our destination, Earth. We are at your experimental supplemental circle location number one, Southern England. The Earth date is August 2001. The coordinate transformation they call altitude is one thousand feet.

"Shall I energize the drafting machine, Mason?"

"Not yet. It's dark, and raining too hard for me to see where to place the pattern. Move backward in time to before it was raining so hard."

The clouds cleared and then I told HAL to stop at this time dimension. I oriented the pattern and told HAL to energize the drafting machine. I fired the machine and saw the energy template form a huge array of circles appear over the field.

"Move ahead in time to after the rainstorm so I can see if the energy pattern imprinted." HAL did, and I saw bright sunlight on a spectacular galaxy of 409 different sized circles. The pattern was about a quarter mile across.

I thought, *Dr. Ev's 8.6 programmers made a design of such complexity that Earthlings will spend years figuring out all the mathematical relationships.*

"HAL, We have twenty patterns to deploy over what the Earthlings perceive as twenty years. Let's go to preprogrammed site number two which is in the year 2005 in what Earthlings consider time."

The pattern that imprinted was a sunburst with four circles in the middle and twenty-seven wavy lines radiating outward. I thought, *That will surely stump the Earthling imposters. Those wavy lines are all precisely alike and cannot be made using of pieces of circles.*

After all twenty of the patterns were imprinted, HAL said, "This concludes our programmed mission. Is there anything else you'd like to do before we transit back to the Vehicle Laboratory?"

I said, "No, I think we've created enough material to keep Earthlings entertained and challenged for many of what they perceive as years."

"Then this concludes our Earth mission 8-514, Advanced Crop Circle Creation. We'll be returning to the laboratory now. It's been a pleasure to have you aboard Mission 8-514 today. We hope you've had a pleasant trip and will travel with us again. Please check your seatbelt as we'll experience some turbulence as we change dimensions. The pod door will open as soon as it's safe to disembark."

CHAPTER 35

The Circle Maker

At breakfast, Kate introduced an overnight arrival at the bed and breakfast, Emma Alberink, from the Netherlands. Kate said, "Emma, tell Ravi and Dave what you saw last night."

Emma was a tall, slender blond woman in her thirties, wearing designer jeans and a patterned blouse. She wore no makeup and had a tired, sad look in her eyes.

She said, "After I had checked in here yesterday, I didn't want to sit alone in my room, so I went for a drive. After dark, I parked in a turnout about a kilometer from here to sit and think. I have a lot going on in my life right now. I fell asleep. About eleven o'clock I woke up and saw this yellow light in the distance over a field. I took out my cellphone and started video recording it. Then, I got out of the car to get a better picture. The light bobbed and floated around and then started coming toward me. I kept recording. It passed overhead and then disappeared."

Dave was excited. "Can we see the video?"

They all gathered around and watched over Emma's shoulder as she played the video.

"That's amazing," said Dave. "Can we see it again?"

Emma handed her iPhone to Dave.

Dave and Ravi watched the video again with delight.

"Can I get a copy of this?" asked Dave.

"Why not?" commented Emma.

"To be fair, I'll pay for it. I'm a lawyer and will write a fair contract for it right now. The contract will allow you to sell it to other people. Is a hundred pounds payment okay?"

Emma looked flustered, thought a minute, smiled, and said, "Fair enough! The money will come in handy for my holiday here."

Dave asked Katie for a pad of paper and a pen. He began to write out a simple contract.

Ravi told Emma, "We appreciate this. Our boss back home wanted us to investigate ball lightning. He'll be delighted if we return with a video of a real sighting. What was the weather like when you took the pictures? Was there any lightning or rain? Did you hear, feel, or smell anything?"

"It was overcast, but nothing else was going on. I didn't feel anything as it passed over me."

"Do you think you could show us where you parked?" Ravi asked.

Emma paused. "I don't think so. I only remember that it was on the side of a hill where the road curved."

Kate interrupted and said, 'I'll bet I know where it was. There aren't many turnouts on the road near here. Was there a white gate and a dirt trail leading up the hill from the turnout?"

"Yes," said Emma. "I remember seeing the gate as I turned the car around. I wondered where the trail went."

The door opened as Elise came into the dining room. She looked around the room, saw Dave writing and Ravi talking to Emma. "What's going on?" she asked.

Ravi introduced Emma and explained the exciting find of the video. Emma showed the video to Elise, who said, "That's quite a development. That's the best video of ball lightning I've ever seen."

"Can we see if we can find the site where she saw it?" Ravi asked.

"Of course. Emma, can you come along.?"

Emma grinned. "Yes. I would love a little distraction now."

Dave transferred Emma's video to his phone, explained the contract, had her sign it and gave her the money.

Emma now had a large smile! She thought, *I didn't expect all this attention.*

Elise said, "Let's all get going. The four of us can fit in my car." She thought, *I don't like this. We might discover something that I'm supposed to avoid.*

They found the turnout and parked. Everyone got out of the car and looked around.

"This is the place," said Emma. "That's the white gate. My car was parked over here, pointed this way."

Dave took out his iPhone. "Would you go over that again so I can make a video of your description?" After she had repeated herself, Dave asked, "Where do you think the ball was when first you saw it?"

Emma pointed downhill. "In that direction."

"That's the barge canal down there, and the road we walked to go to The Barge Inn," said Ravi.

Elise pulled her birding binoculars from the car glove box, studied the field, and said, "I can't see any disturbance to the crops. But, it is hard to tell from this angle. I'll ask the guys who fly the ultralights to check it out in the morning.

"Let's hike higher up this dirt trail and see if we can spot any circles." suggested Dave.

"It is a beautiful day for a hike," added Ravi. "Emma, a hike might make you feel better."

"I agree," said Emma with a smile.

When they returned an hour later, Elise said, "Right now, we are going to Avebury. Emma, would you like to come along? I've also arranged to have lunch with one of the circle making artists."

"Yes. I've heard about the crop circle artists. I'd love to go."

On their way to Avebury, they drove down Kennet Avenue, along the avenue of standing stones, over the thirty-foot deep henge into the center of the thousand-foot diameter circles. The Red Lion Restaurant sat at a crossroads. Elise parked and said, "I see Harry Brighton sitting at one of the picnic tables." Harry was about thirty years old, with black hair. He had an athletic look about him and wore a brown, tweed jacket with blue denim jeans.

Elise said, "He's the circle artist we're supposed to meet." After introductions, they went inside, ordered sandwiches, bought mugs of beer, and went back outside to their table.

Ravi was looking around. "It's beautiful here. Look at the sheep grazing in the fields among the stones and on the sides of the henge that circles the village."

Harry sat next to Emma. Ravi nudged Dave and whispered, "They seem to be hitting it off."

"Harry why don't you tell us how you became a circle artist," said Elise.

Harry began. "Even though I majored in mathematics at University, I'm a graphic artist by trade. I have a small studio in Hanselwood, a village north of here. As a teenager, I became intrigued by the circles Doug and Dave were making. I decided I could make better patterns. I started drawing patterns on paper using only a compass and straight edge.

Dave commented, "The crop circles we have visited were made of straight lines and parts of circles."

"A few friends and I started going into wheat fields at dark and making crop circles" Harry continued. "Our tools are quite simple. We have a surveyor's measuring tape which is attached to a pole or held by one of our team members. Another team member holds onto the other end and tramps the wheat down using a foot board as he moves around the circle."

"The crop circles we visited are precisely drawn. How do you achieve such accuracy?" Dave asked.

"Years of practice. Because we only have about five hours of darkness to hide our efforts, we started with simple patterns. Over time, we've become more efficient and can make larger, more complicated designs. Always, the figures in the fields are made up of circles, segments of circles, and straight lines.

"Over time, other people started making crop circles for various reasons. There are several groups now, all using the same techniques and equipment. One team uses a lawn roller to speed up the work."

"We visited several circles this week. Which did you make?" Ravi asked.

Harry said, "Our small circle-making community is very competitive. However, we have an agreement not to claim authorship of the circles.

"Why did you do that?" asked Dave.

"First of all, we don't want farmers to sue us or have us arrested for damaging crops or trespassing. Secondly, many local people make a living from tourism. We don't want to make them mad. "

"That sounds like a god idea," said Dave

"Also, I've stood in circles I made the night before and confessed to the locals that I made them.. They didn't believe me. The Croppies seem to be content with pretending our circle making community doesn't exist."

"Do you get paid for making the circles?" Dave inquired.

"Yes and no," replied Harry. "Occasionally, people seek us out to make a circle for a television show to prove crop circles are just a hoax. I get jobs from firms that hire and fly my whole crew to some other country to make circles advertising some product or event. One local farmer hires me every year or two to make a circle that he charges tourists to visit.

"I don't get paid for most of the circles I make. It seems to be something I feel I must do. Some nights, a little voice inside my head compels me to go out and make a circle. Maybe, it's the artist in me."

"Are all of the crop circles man-made?" Dave asked.

Harry considered the question for a minute and then countered with, "Do you want them to be?"

Dave replied, "No. I guess it's a scientific question."

Harry said, "To people who believe they are all a hoax, they are all man-made. To people who study them scientifically, most are man-made, but some can't be explained."

"What do you think?" asked Dave.

Ravi thought, *He's not slipping into his usual lawyer cross-examination mode.*

Harry's eyes became a little glassy as he looked into the distance. "Many patterns appear that are far too complex for anyone I know to survey out and make in five hours. Some of those showed up before any of us had even begun to develop our skills and methods. None of us knows how those crop circles were made."

Elise thought, *We don't want to go there.* She decided she'd change the topic. "Harry, have you had any experience with ball lightning?"

"I've seen it from a distance several times. I think it occurs in stormy conditions. We don't work during the weather conditions when they appear."

Emma spoke up, "Harry, I videoed ball lightning on my iPhone last night. Would you like to see it?" She was reaching into her coat pocket.

Harry looked delighted as he said, "Absolutely!"

Elise said, "We're about to go into town and do some sightseeing. Harry, would you like to come along?"

Harry replied, "I would like to study this video."

Emma looked at Harry. "I've visited Avebury before. I'll stay here and go over the video with you, Harry, if you'll give me a ride back to the bed and breakfast I'm staying at."

Harry smiled. "Happy to do it. It's on my way home. Would you like another pint?"

"We'll see you later," said Dave.

After they had played tourist in Avebury, Elise started driving them back to the bed and breakfast. "What time is your plane tomorrow?"

"Five-thirty in the afternoon," answered Dave. "But we need to get there about three-thirty. We're supposed to have a video conference with our boss in California after we're checked in."

Elise mentally reviewed her calendar and then said, "I'm afraid I have a doctor's appointment that will interfere with me taking you to the airport. I'll have one of my friends drive you if that's okay."

"Could we hire a cab or something?" asked Dave.

"No need to bother. I'll arrange someone. Getting you to the airport on time is part of the tour package. Have you achieved your goals in coming here?"

Dave looked at Ravi and said, "Indeed. Getting the video of the ball lightning was a real plus. We appreciate how you exposed us to various people's views of who makes crop circles and why."

Elise thought, *I'll see if I can't get some short quote for my official report to MI6.* "As a scientist, did you reach any conclusions as to whether some crop circles are of made by non-human intelligence?"

Dave thought a minute and then said, "I believe you asked that question of me as a lawyer and scientist. I would have to answer the question by saying I found nothing I would call hard evidence to support the idea of non-human intelligence involvement."

Elise thought, *That's a relief.* Then she asked Ravi, "What did you conclude?"

Ravi said, "I'm with Dave in his summary. We didn't see any aliens or UFOs. I did observe some unusual energies in one crop circle, but that doesn't mean it came from aliens. With or without UFOs, we have enjoyed our trip here."

"I'm glad to hear that," replied Elise.

"One more thing to add," said Dave. "I conclude crop circles are like magic mirrors that reflect your beliefs. What you expect to experience or see is there. I had no fixed expectations so I could evaluate the opinions of the people you put us in contact with without prejudice."

After a pause, Elise said, "I must say, that's a viewpoint I've never heard."

Ravi thought, *This is terrific! He's not looking at things only as a lawyer or scient*ist anymore. He's speaking from the heart.

Ravi spoke, "And we enjoyed hiking in the English countryside. I'll have those beautiful, rolling, wheat fields and the cows and sheep grazing in my memory for a long time. We appreciate how you introduced us to so many colorful people. This has truly been a vacation to another land."

After they had stopped at the bed and breakfast, Ravi and Dave both gave Elise unexpected hugs and said goodbye. As she drove away, Elise thought, *Wonderful. They're not going home with any substantiated beliefs that aliens are involved with crop circles. They're not going home with any solid information about ball lightning! I'll file my official report to Charlie tomorrow. Daniel Hughes at MI6 will be delighted!*

CHAPTER 36

One Last Circle

"It's our last night in England. We should do something special. Let's walk on the road through the wheat field and up the canal to The Barge Inn. I'd like one more mug of Area 51 cider."

Dave smiled at Ravi and then replied, "I agree. I think I would like another mug of their Alien Abduction Green Beer to protect me on the flight home. Maybe I'll buy us a couple of their tin-foil hats for our further protection."

As they walked along the dirt road through the wheat field, Ravi said, "This is a beautiful time of night! Look at how the yellow light shines on the green field."

Dave stopped, grabbed Ravi's hand, pointed and said, "Look over there! I saw a light in the middle of the field. It might be ball lightning." He pulled out his iPhone and took some pictures.

Ravi pulled on Dave's hand. "We can go down these tractor tracks and get closer. Look! It seems to be coming this way."

Dave stopped, took more pictures, and said, "Let's stand still so I can video it. It's coming right at us!"

"Somehow I don't feel frightened," said Ravi.

The bright ball stopped about one-hundred feet away and then bobbed up and down.

"I'm getting some great footage here. It seems to be inviting us to follow."

He took Ravi's hand as they walked toward the light. It moved slowly. They followed it about a hundred yards until it moved away from the track, over the wheat.

"Shall we follow it? Look! It stopped. It's fading out! I have it all on video."

It was gone.

Dave turned to Ravi and said, "I think we should walk through the wheat and check out where it disappeared. Stay behind me so we won't make too wide a trail through the farmer's wheat, okay?"

They plodded through the wheat for a minute and then Ravi said, "Look, we're in a crop circle!"

Dave marveled, "It's only about thirty feet in diameter. It has all the hallmarks of the real circle I read about. The wheat is laid down in an elaborate weave of many layers. Did you notice that the only trail into the circle is the one made by us?" He continued taking pictures.

Ravi got her dowsing rods out of her pack and started doing a toe-heel shuffle and quietly chanting as she moved around the periphery of the circle. Her dowsing rods swung one way and another as she moved. "Look at the energy here!" she exclaimed, "The field reverses every foot I move."

"What is that chant?" asked Dave.

"It's a Native American song my grandmother in Santa Fe taught me. This is so exciting!"

Dave was down on his knees examining the weave of the wheat in the flattened areas. "In this little area," he observed, "I can see that the wheat has seven layers, woven together, each pointing a different way."

Raving shuffled around the interior of the circle, and announced, "The dowsing rods point in seven different directions as I move around the circle."

After excitedly examining the circle for a few minutes, they both sat down at the edge of the circle. They laughed after they said in unison, "This is the real thing!"

Ravi said, "When we first came to England, I believed all crop circles were one big hoax. I believe this one is real!"

She turned to Dave and pulled him on top of her. They held a long kiss and then Ravi moved her head away and stared into his eyes. As she continued to kiss him she started unbuttoning his shirt and said in a low voice, "The lady channeling to her tour group said we should experience the circles with our whole being. Have you ever done or had a Croppie?"

CHAPTER 37

Report to Colson

After checking in at the Heathrow ticket counter, they were standing in the security line when Dave's cell phone rang. "Yes," he answered, "we are going through security now. We can be there in fifteen minutes or so. We have a lot to report. Okay. Goodbye."

He turned to Ravi and said, "We don't have to video conference with Colson. He's here in the first class lounge. He just happened to be passing through. Yesterday, he found out from his California office that we'd be here at the same time. We're going to meet him as soon as we leave security."

"He sure gets around," commented Ravi.

"What a surprise to see you here," said Dave to Vince Colson as they shook hands.

Vince looked at Ravi and said, "You both are looking great. Madam Associate Director, you are positively beaming."

"That's what a few days hiking through the English countryside can do," replied Ravi, who truly felt like she was radiating light.

"Vince, we had a close encounter with ball lightning last night. It seemed to drift around. It led us to a unique crop circle. I captured it all on video on my cell phone."

Dave showed and narrated the videos he had taken to Vince, including the videos documenting the crop circle.

"We're quite certain that ball lightning is real but inexplicable. It seemed to be at an ambient temperature since it didn't burn anything it touched. It floated about six feet above the ground."

Vince looked perplexed and said, "I didn't expect this. You two are thorough investigators. I think your discovery could have implications I didn't anticipate. I met with one of my British contacts yesterday. He became concerned when I told him about your investigation. You've apparently stumbled into something highly classified by the British government."

"Are they going to get us for being spies?" asked Ravi with fear in her voice.

"No but I'm afraid I'll have to show these videos to him before anyone else sees them, or we talk to anyone about them. For now, we should treat them as a highly proprietary trade secret. Has anyone else seen them?"

"No, I shot these videos last night."

"Good," said Vince, "I'm not concerned about the video the lady you called Emma made. It was shot at a distance and is easily dismissed as a fake. Please transmit your videos to my iPhone now.

Then, do a secure erase of all your copies. Don't keep anything. It might lead to serious trouble later."

As they sat there, Dave sent the videos to Vince and then did a secure delete of the files. Dave thought, *I think he means **serious trouble**. I'd better distance myself from this.*

Vince said, "Okay I have the files. I'll take them to my British friend this afternoon. Remember, not a word to anyone about the ball lightning or what you experienced in the crop circle."

Ravi thought, *I'm glad we didn't tell him about our Croppie.*

Dave said, "I understand. None of it ever happened. In some of my high-profile patent and trade secret cases, we had situations like this. I've attended many meetings that didn't happen.'"

Vince stopped looking concerned as he put his cell phone away and said, "Understand, I'm delighted I sent you over here and that you did such a complete investigation. Very professional! Your findings will be valuable to me. A great return on my investment. I hope you enjoyed conducting the investigation."

Dave thought, *Some circles were better than others.*

Ravi mused, *You wouldn't believe. . . .*

Vince smiled and thought. *This video may be my ticket to full access to the Dragonfly program. It's probably a gold mine of technology.*

CHAPTER 38

Mason's Final Exam

It was time for my final exam. I created a small amphitheater with tiered rows of dark wood seats silhouetted in front of a soft white background. I sat on a stage with Dr. Oz standing at a podium nearby. The elders filed in, wearing white robes, took seats, and filled the room with a sense of serious concern. The Principal Elder spoke in a thunderous, deep, echoing voice. "Dr. Oz, you may begin."

"Our middle school student is here to report on his science project," he said pointing at me. "He completed his Earthlings 1a course and excelled at making Earth-like illusions and communicating with an assigned pair of Earthlings. I'll let him create the illusions he has selected to illustrate his study of Earth and Earthlings."

I moved to the podium and created a large screen behind me upon which I projected two-dimensional images.

I said, "This is like a primitive communication apparatus Earthlings use in meetings such as this. They call it power-point."

I narrated the geological evolution of the granite mountains and ice fields. I narrated the flow of history showing the evolution of tribes and their wars and conflicts. I described my interaction with the Dave and Raven pair.

I heard the elders murmuring. The Principal observed, "We noticed a strange energy flow between the pair."

I replied, "They call it love."

The Principal commented, "We sense that you could perceive it while you were interacting."

"I did, during some parts of our interaction."

The Principal said, "I don't believe any of us has had any experience with that type of energy." He asked the other elders, "Have we ever experienced it on any of the other civilizations we have studied?" There was a pause and then the Principal stated, "None of our group has found that experience. Please proceed."

Dr. Oz took the podium and said, "For his Earthlings 1a Science Project, the student worked under Dr. Ev and perceptually traveled to Earth in one of his automated pods. On Earth, they have areas of vegetation called wheat fields. The student caused earth energies to make patterns in the fields and then studied the Earthlings' response to them. The student will show you."

I returned to the podium and turned the two-dimensional illusion back on. I narrated as I showed the distribution of the patterns in space-time and the evolution of earthling responses. I showed how Earthlings appeared to form tribes centered on their beliefs about the source and meaning of the circles. I summarized how my subject pair responded to the circles. The elders were puzzled by my last scene of Ravi and Dave in the moonlight crop circle.

Dr. Oz returned to the podium and said, "This concludes the student presentation. Please advise if he should proceed on to Earthlings 2 and what his assignment should be."

The Principal said in a booming voice, "Thank you, student. That was a commendable presentation. We will now retire to deliberate."

All of the seats were emptied. Dr. Oz disappeared. I started to get apprehensive, but suddenly everyone was back. (Remember, on our planet, time is only an illusion.)

The Principal spoke in deep echoing syllables. "You may continue to Earthlings 2. For your assignment, your spirit will be code named Mason. It will incarnate into thirteen bodies living in different eras of Earth space and time. Your destiny in each of those lives will be an exploration of the various forms of the energy you called Love. After all of those lives are ended, you will return to this forum. You will be assigned an upper-class being to be your guide. Any questions?"

After a brief pause, the elders and the amphitheater disappeared with a whooshing sound.

I was left standing on the stage, alone except for the feeling of another entity being present. "Are you my guide? Let's manifest as human bodies since that is the media we will be working in."

I manifested myself as a ten-year-old boy wearing jeans and a T-shirt and said, "The elder's said my earth code name is Mason. You can call me that for now. I understand I will have many names and bodies."

The entity manifested itself as an old, gray-haired woman in a flowing white robe who said, "This appearance may be appropriate. In most lives, you will not be aware of me. I will always be there to protect and telepathically advise you."

"Do you have an earth name?" I asked.

"You will know me by many names."

"Okay, Many Names, how did you get this assignment?"

"We've something in common. When I was doing the Earthlings 1a course, I experimented with ball lightning. I'm now doing Earthlings 3. You're my freshman high school psychology experiment."

"Now, it's time for us to audition parents who embrace the belief systems that will guide you on the life experience of what you call love.

"Since in our reality, time does not exist, all of your thirteen lives will be concurrent. They will only be spread out in time-space coordinates in Earth's reality. No lifetime will precede another.

"There will be bleed-throughs between lives. In any one of your lives, you may receive pictures, beliefs, thoughts or emotions from one of your lives at another time coordinate. In earth terms, they call these past or future lifetimes. You will also meet other beings who are playing roles in several of your incarnations. The bleed-throughs allow you to integrate the experience of the same subject, in your case love, in all thirteen incarnations.

"The experiences I've planned so far are: bondage instead of love, obligation instead of love, lust instead of love, love as loss, friendship instead of love, conditional love, and unconditional love. We can think up more as we select your thirteen experiences."

"May I pick some of my parents?" asked Mason.

"Of course. You get to pick them all. Let's audition this couple in Earth time 1602 I've found. They believe that females are slaves. You can choose either the male or female role. I think the experience of this lifetime will be 'bondage instead of love.'"

With that thought, Mason hurriedly said, "I think I'd like to start with Earth-time 2016 and 'unconditional love.'"

The illusion Many Names had created started to fade as he said, "Take me to the first parents you'd like to choose."

179

CHAPTER 39

The Proof

The doorbell of their Playa Vista apartment rang.

"Honey, would you get that? I can't get up." Ravi said as she struggled to get to a sitting position on the couch.

"Only one month to go," said Dave as he headed to the door."

"Will Easter or the spring solstice ever get here?" moaned Ravi holding her bulging belly.

Dave returned unwrapping a FedEx package. "It's from your publisher!"

"The final proof of my book! It also gestated too long."

Dave weighed the manuscript in his hand. "Is it done? I was amazed by how fast you wrote the book once you got started. Are you finally going to let me read it?" asked Dave.

"Absolutely! Even I can't change it much now."

Dave sat down next to Ravi, held her hand, and read aloud:

"Call me Mason, even though I don't have a name as you know it. I'm communicating with you from another planet that your civilization has not yet found. Some years ago, even though time is an illusion, I was a student starting a middle school course series called Earthlings.

Dave stopped reading and asked, "Is this yours?

Ravi answered, "After I started writing, the text simply flowed out of my subconscious. I sometimes felt I was only editing the book–not writing it. Some of it seemed to be coming from another place–like the future."

Dave continued reading.

"Come with me on a journey to explore many versions of the story of love."

Ravi blurted out, "The only part I'm positive was mine is the last page. Turn to the last line."

Dave thumbed through the pages and then read,

"Mason appeared before the Presidium of elders giving the student report on his experience of thirteen lives as an earthling. At the end of the report Mason said:

"The grandest thing I ever learned in these human lifetimes is how to love and be loved in return."

Dave looked at Ravi and saw the largest, most wonderful smile he had ever seen.

About Ken Renshaw

Ken Renshaw made a lifelong study of recognizing the beliefs and patterns in peoples' lives. This led him to write a book, "The Secret of Your Life Script" about how beliefs and life scripts make the same things happen to us over and over.

Then, Ken Renshaw tackled a really big belief. He'd always had certain secret psychic abilities and ESP (which were most useful in business). But he could never talk about these things in the presence of other scientists or engineers. They had strong beliefs against the validity of any phenomena that did not fit their scientific paradigms. So, Ken set out to create a scientific explanation of ESP phenomena. The product of all this thinking is Ken Renshaw's book, "Science, Remote Viewing and ESP: Beyond Einstein's Horizon."

Ken made an updated and simplified version of that book in a Kindle format, "A Friendly Guide to ESP and Remote Viewing."

Ken Renshaw decided that we are entangled in a psychic web of life that can extend over past lives and space and time which can guide our everyday existence. Some call it The Matrix

Ken graduated with a Bachelor of Science in Electrical Engineering from Stanford in 1960. He worked his way through school as a Research Associate in the Radiophysics Laboratory, studying the ionosphere, counting meteors, and leading a scientific expedition in the North Atlantic to measure man-made aurora borealis. Ken has applied his knowledge of radio and other electromagnetic phenomena to understanding the physics of ESP.

He retired as a Chief Scientist at Hughes Aircraft. He was a "Rocket Scientist" and designed and sold communication satellites to telephone companies.

Ken lives with the love of his life, Joyce, at the edge of a pine forest, overlooking the ocean, listening to the sound of the surf, in Cambria, California.